Mary Wesley was born near Windsor in 1912. Her education took her to the London School of Economics and during the War she worked in the War Office. She has also worked part-time in the antique trade. Mary Wesley has lived in London, France, Italy, Germany and several places in the West Country. She now lives 'rather a hermit's existence' in Devon. She has previously written for children and comments that her 'chief claim to fame is arrested development, getting my first novel published at the age of seventy' That first novel was *Jumping the Queue*. Her later novels, *The Camomile Lawn, Harnessing Peacocks, The Vacillations of Poppy Carew*, and *Not That Sort of Girl* are also published by Black Swan.

Author photograph by Kate Ganz Dorment.

Also by Mary Wesley

JUMPING THE QUEUE
THE CAMOMILE LAWN
HARNESSING PEACOCKS
THE VACILLATIONS OF POPPY CAREW
NOT THAT SORT OF GIRL

and published by Black Swan

Second Fiddle

Mary Wesley

BLACK SWAN

SECOND FIDDLE

A BLACK SWAN BOOK 0 552 99355 7

Originally published in Great Britain
by Macmillan London Limited

PRINTING HISTORY

Macmillan edition published 1988
Black Swan edition published 1989

This book is set in 11/13 pt Mallard
by Colset Private Limited, Singapore.

Black Swan Books are published by Transworld Publishers Ltd., 61–63 Uxbridge Road, Ealing, London W5 5SA, in Australia by Transworld Publishers (Australia) Pty. Ltd., 15–23 Helles Avenue, Moorebank, NSW 2170, and in New Zealand by Transworld Publishers (N.Z.) Ltd., Cnr. Moselle and Waipareira Avenues, Henderson, Auckland.

Made and printed in Great Britain by
The Guernsey Press Co. Ltd.,
Guernsey, Channel Islands.

For Robert Bolt

PART I

Autumn

Claud Bannister sat beside his mother, enduring the concert.

What right, he asked himself, had an unknown provincial quartet to perform three pieces of modern music for the first time? How was a discriminating sophisticate such as himself to know whether the music was good or bad? I need, he told himself with secret mortification, to read the opinion of the London critics before I dare judge. I am ignorant of music, if not tone deaf. I am neither discriminating nor sophisticated; I have come back to Mother after years of school, university and failed exams without money or qualifications, without even the courage to tell her what I intend to do with my life. What shall I say when she asks me? This music is incomprehensible, he thought, glancing covertly at his mother, yet she seems to understand it. What does she hear which I do not?

On the way to the concert Margaret Bannister had tried, unwisely she now realised, to jolly her son out of his gloomy mood and, failing, had called him 'a veritable bundle of resentment' – another of her misplaced remarks, she told herself, exasperated. To hell with it, she would enjoy the music, worry later.

These seats are appallingly uncomfortable, thought

Claud, leaning back until the back of his seat creaked, tangibly annoying a bald man sitting in the row behind, a man who as they had come in to the concert hall had called out to his mother in jest, laughed appreciatively at some negligible joke she had made in return, had obviously admired her and been backed in his opinion by his wife who, grey-haired, stout and dowdy, had kindly included him, Claud, with, 'How nice to see you, Claud' (remembering his name while he remotely forgot hers). 'How seldom we see you, how glad you must be to spend some time with your clever, witty mother.'

Clever? Witty? What did all these grey old people know of cleverness or wit?

The quartet scraped to the end of the difficult piece. The audience clapped, the musicians stood and bowed.

'I might grow to like it when I have listened to it a few more times,' his mother said to the neighbour on her left. 'We finish, thank the Lord, with dear old Bach but they did their best, the brave young things.'

Claud scowled at the quartet, stringy and not particularly young, bracing themselves to have a bash at Bach while his mother sat back relaxed, anticipating pleasure. Grey, grey, they are all grey, grey-haired and largely dressed in grey. Claud's eyes roamed disapprovingly over the audience, seeing grey even when the heads were tinted black, auburn, even blond.

His eye was arrested by the sight of a woman three rows ahead, dressed in vivid green, a striped wrap in cyclamen and purple lit with blue slung round her shoulders. He could make out a white neck and above it a shock of dark springy hair; by leaning forward he could just make out a pointed nose and one dark eye.

'Who is that?' he whispered in his parent's ear. 'What's her name?'

'Hush, I will introduce you presently.' That his mother should know on the instant the only person in the audience who was of interest to him added to Claud's sulks. He leaned back in his uncomfortable seat, letting the Bach flow, feeding his resentment (what a bloody evening), disgustedly anticipating the soggy quiches and mediocre wines which would be distributed by benign ladies ('White wine or red? Or *rosé*? We have *rosé*, soft drinks too, of course') while their husbands collected donations for the charity in aid of which the concert had been organised. Claud glared at his mother, who was smiling as though amused. What's funny about a boring provincial concert? It's probably in aid of some wretched cretins who would have been happier if allowed to die at birth.

He was presently introduced to the woman in green in the foyer among a babble of voices. She stood with a piece of quiche in one hand and a glass of wine in the other, talking with her mouth full to the conductor of the cacophony they had just listened to.

Claud heard her say, 'You know, I simply *loathe* modern music.' She sprayed crumbs from a full-lipped mouth, caught Claud's eye briefly, looked away, said, 'Hullo, Margaret,' leaned forward to kiss his mother's cheek – 'I'm spewing crumbs, sorry' – and turned back to the conductor who, Claud remarked jealously, was a darkly attractive foreigner. Margaret Bannister turned, laughing, to speak to friends, leaving Claud to hover and snatch his chance when the guest of honour would be wrested away to be introduced to others. Knowing his mother, he guessed that he would, if lucky, have seven minutes to make his mark before she insisted on leaving. In the event he had ten.

'He's Roumanian,' said Claud's mother, as they moved away towards the car. 'He probably thinks Laura pronounces love, loathe. She will risk insulting people in public, it's the sort of joke which appeals to her.'

'Is she a tough cookie?'

'I suspect a heart of nougat. Would you like to drive?'

Claud guessed rightly that his parent was sick of his ill humour and ready to placate him. Had they reached the moment when he dared apprise her of his future plans? He got behind the steering wheel.

'You should have more confidence in your driving,' said his mother presently, as he braked violently at a crossroads.

'By which you mean I should have more confidence in myself?' Claud accelerated, hating the oblique criticism which, he now told himself, had driven his father into leaving home. His mother did not reply. This kind of silence had also precipitated his father's departure. We have not reached the right moment, he told himself.

Laura Thornby accepted another glass of wine but refused the quiche. She stood with her back to the wall, watching the concert crowd thin as they said their goodbyes, collected their wraps and went out into the night where the timbre of their voices sharpened in the freezing air. She thought, as the concert hall doors opened and shut, that she must have imagined the shiver of apprehension she had felt when Margaret Bannister introduced her son. She had felt the draught, she told herself, the night outside was freezing. Her shiver was nothing to do with Claud Bannister.

What a lot he had said in those short minutes. How impetuous to spill such a lapful of hope and ambition to a stranger. What a risk he had taken. And in a crowd! Anyone could have heard what he said. Sipping her wine Laura waited for the evening to end and as she waited she thought of Claud Bannister and was interested in her interest.

'Can we give you a lift?' Helen Peel, her arm through her husband's, slowed as they walked by.

'No, thank you. I have my car.'

'Someone said you brought the conductor down from London,' said Helen's husband Christopher.

'I did, but he is going back by train.'

'So you will be down for a few days?'

'Probably.'

'What's his name again, this conductor?' asked Christopher.

'Composer,' corrected Helen.

'Both.' Laura smiled at Helen.

'D'you mean he wrote that stuff, then conducted it?' Christopher towered over Laura. 'You do find yourself the most curious boyfriends.'

'So you did not like it.'

'Not much. Well, not at all. I'm not up to this modern stuff.'

'People said the same about Mozart. Come on, Christopher, we shall be—' Helen started to move.

'But what's his name? I've lost my programme and came without my glasses.'

'Clug,' said Laura.

'Clug?'

'To rhyme with plug.'

'Oh! Oh, all right darling, I'm coming.' Christopher Peel allowed himself to be led away. 'Is the fellow a Communist?' he asked over his shoulder.

'Probably.'

'– wouldn't be allowed out of Roumania if he were not.'

Helen belonged to the class of English women who are taught to elocute clearly at an early age, thought Laura, listening to Helen's voice calling back, 'Goodnight,' as she and her husband went out into the cold.

Waiting for Clug to free himself of admirers Laura speculated idly on the gap there would be in her life with Clug returned to Roumania. It had been an agreeable intermezzo, she thought, of just the right length, no time to get bored.

'Are you delivering Clug to British Rail?' The county artistic director came up now. 'If it's a nuisance I can easily—'

'No, no, Robert, everything's okay, his bags are in my car. It's no bother.'

The artistic director wondered whether he should say something about Clug stopping the night in Salisbury on the way down to see the sights? Perhaps he had better not since Laura appeared to have been with him – well, she had driven him down, hadn't she? Not that that necessarily meant—'I think the concert was a success,' he said, looking doubtfully at the thinning crowd, finding Laura slightly alarming.

'Of course it was. D'you think you could extract him from that hive of music lovers? He will miss his train otherwise.'

'Of course, of course. I don't think they are as much musicologists as – well – ah – he's a very attractive chap, isn't he? I'll do a bit of tactful disentanglement, shall I?'

Robert shot off to detach the conductor, who stood surrounded by an eager group of women and less eager men.

Laura waved in the direction of Clug, caught his eye, tapped her watch. Clug waved back and put his arm round rescuing Robert's shoulder.

After a while Clug leaned back in the car beside Laura. 'Ach, that's good. That boy look at you with calf eye, I see it.'

'*Saw* him,' said Laura, 'not *it*.' She turned up the heater. 'And it's calves' eyes, not calf. What have you been reading, Cluggie?'

'Woman's magazine. I try to learn all about loathing in capitalismus countries. So much freedom. Now in my country—'

'Loving, Clug, loving. I can't think why I bother.'

Clug chuckled. 'I go 'ome, so no problem, darling. Loathe, love, same thing.'

'Good job you are going.'

'So you no longer loathe me?' Clug queried.

'Might be verging on it.'

'I observe cruel tone of voice. No need to understand worts.'

'Crotchets and quavers.'

'Comment?'

'My French is as weak as your English.'

'You squash. Come to Bucharest,' Clug cajoled. 'A nice little visit. I fix visa.'

'No, thank you. I have told you. No fear.'

'Notting to fear.'

'Oh God,' Laura exclaimed irritably, 'do shut up just for once. No fear is slang, it means no thank you, nothing doing.'

'We do not do enough,' Clug laughed.

'Did not.'

'Okay, did not. So why not come now? Jost one last night?'

'No. *Non. Nein. Niet.*'

'*Niet*, I understand.'

'That's great. Now here's the station. Got your ticket? Got your bag?'

'You come?'

'No, I told you.'

'So – you – did.' If he wished, if he made the effort, a few words could be accentless. 'So a kiss, a final kiss?'

Laura pulled on the handbrake, leaned over and kissed his cheek. 'Goodbye, Cluggie.'

'Do not get hurted by that calf boy.'

'The boot might be on the other foot.'

'Yes, that also.' He was out of the car now, turning up his coat collar, yanking his suitcase from the boot of the car. 'In so situation two get hurt. You betray or he betray.'

Laura was out of the car, standing beside him. 'I can't see anything reaching that stage.' She was amused. 'You foresee a non-event.'

'You do not see much. Let me stay your place tonight or you come to London?'

'No, Cluggie, I told you. I have to see my family, go to the dentist—'

'I would like to see your home.'

'Lovers are apt to get bitten.'

'Is it so convention, your familia?'

'If you don't buck up, you will miss your train.'

The train, said the man at the barrier, was ten minutes late. Clug put his bag on a seat and, taking Laura's arm, started walking her up and down the platform. Constrained by good manners to see him safely onto the train, Laura sighed. She was looking forward to getting into bed by herself; she found this extra delay an imposition.

'Little Laura.' Clug squeezed Laura's arm against his ribs (they were of a height). ' 'ow I shall miss you, for me you represent all that is in this country er - er—'

'You have already forgotten what I represent.'

'No, no I 'ave not.' Clug's aitches froze as they left his lips. 'I shall even remember your great uncles, the most lovely uncles in Western Europe.'

'Ankles, Cluggie, ankles.'

'Votever. When I feel them wrapped round my vaiste I adore them, get most excite, ant your viggling toes, now this young calf will experience this extase.'

Catching the eye of a man supposedly reading the evening paper, Laura grinned. 'Work that one out, mate.' The stranger raised his newspaper, blotting himself away.

'So now this and that with that young so lucky fellow, to start so with a beautiful older woman is bonus,' cried Clug. 'And a so fonny woman also.'

'I'm not starting anything, Cluggie, I'm due for a little rest.'

'Rest! Nah! If he start it is better, but it vill be you, I think, no?'

'I think I hear your train,' said Laura, laughing.

'Do not forget me, little Laura. I vill remember as you are now forever. How we loathed!'

'We look like corpses under this fluorescent light - loved Cluggie, loved. I still can't think why I bother.'

'In Venezia the street lights are pink.'

'And in Bucharest?'

'Like death also.'

'Here's your train. Where's your bag? Goodbye,

goodbye.' Laura's spirits soared as the train arrived; she felt revivified and looked it, in spite of the fluorescent lighting. Clug climbed nimbly into the train.

'I am still working out how you wrapped your uncle's ankles round a waste—' The newspaper reader brushed past Laura and followed Clug onto the train as it began to move.

'Thanks!' Laughing, Laura blew a kiss towards the anonymous humorist. Leaning from the window Clug, taking the kiss to be for him, blew it back.

Walking back to her car Laura was grateful for the note of frivolity which had rescued her in the nick of time from incipient boredom. If I meet Margaret Bannister's son again I shall treat him in paltry fashion, she resolved. Arm's length should be the rule for a while, safety lay in being casual.

As the train gathered speed Martin Bengough, laying his newspaper aside, began to fuss, patting his pockets, opening his briefcase, rustling through its contents, then half standing up as though he might inadvertently have sat on the elusive object he was looking for. Not finding it, he sighed gustily and sat discontentedly in his seat to stare out of the window into the dark. Reflected in the glass he saw himself and his fellow occupants of the carriage as they relaxed and settled down for the journey to London.

A pair of adolescent boys had brought a travelling chess set; two girls travelling together wore Walkmen clamped to their heads. While one chewed gum and read a magazine, the other had brought out her knitting and clicked the needles frenetically. A white-haired old woman sat with her eyes shut, both hands holding her bag. By himself, in a corner seat halfway along the compartment, Clug was absorbed in a musical score.

Five or six burly young men of the type seen travelling to or from football matches barged suddenly through the compartment on their way back from the buffet car, bringing a waft of cold air mingling with the smell of stale tobacco; they each carried several cans of beer and sandwiches encased in plastic. As they lurched past Clug his fingers tightened on the score and he winced into himself, hunching his shoulders and drawing in legs which had been stretched out.

The train swung round a curve on the line; one of the young men lurched against Clug. 'Sorry, squire.' Clug looked up quickly, then down again, his fingers gripping the score. As the football fans clanged and bumped their way out of the compartment they were followed by the ticket collector, a tall Sikh in a blue turban. He took each ticket and examined it in silence before politely returning it to its owner. Taking Clug's ticket he said quietly: 'You are in the wrong compartment, sir, this is a first class ticket.'

'No matter,' said Clug. 'I move if the train crowds too heavy.' The ticket collector returned the ticket and moved on in the wake of the football fans.

Martin, feeling the train begin to slow, stood up, picked up his briefcase and stood by the sliding doors ready to leave the train at the junction which was the last stop before London. The junction platform was crowded with waiting passengers catching this last connection; some of them carried skis.

Martin leaned from the train window, his hand on the heavy brass handle. As the train drew to a halt, he stepped down into the crowd. 'Fifth row facing the engine, right-hand side, feels safer travelling second class,' he said, brushing past a man swinging himself onto the train.

'Oh, the bugger,' said the man without looking at Martin. 'I had looked forward to travelling in comfort.'

Martin grinned and started elbowing his way through the crowd to the exit. As he paused to give up his ticket, he looked back: the train was already moving and he could see his successor through the window standing near Clug, heaving his bag up onto the rack. Clug was studying his score.

Martin strolled out of the station to the car park where his car waited. He was very hungry. The quiche at the concert had been uneatable; he had swerved away from the wine. He looked forward to the meal he had ordered earlier in the day at a small country restaurant not yet recommended by Egon Ronay, run by the friend of an acquaintance who would be ready to oblige with a late meal.

On his way to the restaurant he stopped at a callbox, reported in and registered the fact that he had a few days' leave. 'I have left my umbrella behind,' he said.

'If by that,' said the voice at the other end, 'you mean you are hotfooting after a pussycat—'

'Retrieving my brolly,' said Martin equably. 'It belonged to my grandfather; he bought it pre-war at Briggs, the umbrella makers in Piccadilly, London, SW1.'

'Snob,' said the voice, envying Martin his ancestral umbrella with its malacca handle and gold band with the grandfather's name on it. 'One day it will get nicked,' he said, 'I hope. Don't miss your flight, will you?'

Martin replaced the receiver.

He drove back the way he had come by train then, leaving the main road, found his intended restaurant in a village restored to peace and calm by being bypassed. The restaurant was small and comfortable, several tables still occupied by customers lingering over the debris of their meal. He ate a particularly delicious mussel soup, woodcock with matchstick potatoes, watercress salad, and a plain orange *compôte*. The house wine was so good he wondered whether he could safely drive on. Discovering that there were bedrooms to let above the dining-room, he reserved one, ordered cheese and disposed contentedly of the bottle. Later when he went up to bed he found that the house, which he had not seen in the dark, had once been a mill and that his room was above the mill-race.

He opened a window and peered in the dark at black water channelling towards an obsolete millwheel. Further out the main stream slid over a waterfall to crash into a deep pool. This would be a pleasant place to cast a fly on a June evening, but now the air was icy; he shut the window and got into bed.

Listening to the water he reviewed the evening, the last of assignment Clug. And, since Clug spent so much time with her, he had included Laura in the watching.

At the start of Clug's concert tour, at a reception, he had seen them meet. Noted an instant rapport. Since then Clug and Laura had spent all the time Clug could manage together. It had puzzled him that she should take up with Clug when there could be no future in the liaison. She behaved as he frequently did himself, taking up with a girl for a short term, happy never to see her again. Martin grinned, amused to find this affinity between himself and the woman he had been observing for a month. They had spoken for the first time that evening as he got on the train and she, smiling, had let him know that she had known all along and not cared that he watched her while he watched the Roumanian.

He had done more than watch, he acknowledged to himself. By using the ploy of a mislaid umbrella, he would double back to discover, if he could, more about Laura; he was intrigued by her, fascinated. He could perhaps discover why she lived alone, worked alone, had apparently satisfactory but only short-term relationships. A fellow watcher changing shifts had told him that he had come across Laura before, having an affair on that occasion with a visiting American academician suspected by the CIA of sympathising with Chilean lefties. Another colleague remembered that she had had a brief brush with a Hungarian painter in England, like Clug, on a cultural visit. With both these men she had stayed quite openly in hotels, but paid her own way.

What a futile, sneaky life I lead, thought Martin. He wondered, as he had for many months, whether to chuck his job, find a more congenial occupation, or drift on a little longer? He was supposed to be in Washington by the weekend on a fresh assignment. Should he resign now, as he had already suggested he might to his masters, or after the American tour? He liked Washington. He liked the museums and galleries. It was plain that there was no future in a pursuit of Laura. In the urbane Phillips Gallery, lolling on one of the sofas, he might shed thoughts of Laura Thornby. He particularly liked the Phillips Gallery. Even so, he thought, drifting into sleep to the sound of rushing water, there was no harm in thinking it would be fun to bring Laura to this idyllic place, imagine sharing with her a delicious meal, then bringing her up to this room into this bed. He was wryly amused that in his mid-forties he was still capable of romantic fantasy.

'You are such a sidelong girl,' said Claud, aware that Laura was avoiding his eye. They had been introduced at the concert the previous evening, he reminded her; up to then he had known her by sight only, he said.

'I am in my forties.' Laura, not the sort to be flattered by being called a girl, continued doing what she had been doing when accosted, picking over the vegetables on the organic stall, much to the irritation of the stall-holder. 'If I live to be ninety, which is the current mode, God help us, I am now into middle age.'

'You certainly don't look it,' said Claud, wondering whether the expression 'sidelong' had caused offence.

'One should look one's age,' said Laura, her long fingers pinching garlic bulbs. 'How much – some of these are powdery?' she asked the stall-holder.

The stall-holder weighed the garlic. 'Ninety pee.'

'You don't half charge,' said Laura, returning the garlic to its heap. 'I shall buy the less healthy French kind from my vegetable shop; it's fatter, juicier, fresher, cheaper—'

'Now, now,' said the stall-holder, 'think of the muck it's grown in, sheer poison.'

Claud tried again. 'You have allowed experience to etch those delicate laughter lines,' he suggested, peering at the skin round Laura's eyes.

'That's about it. How much is the broccoli?' she asked the stall-holder.

Claud resisted an inclination to kick Laura on the shin; she was wearing strong leather boots; talking to two people at once bordered, in his book, on bad manners. 'Most women enjoy flattery,' he said.

'I am not most women.' Laura was now picking over the broccoli. 'All right, I'll have a couple of pounds, Brian.' She smiled at the stall-holder.

'What an idea!' exclaimed Claud. 'You are strikingly original.'

'So what shall we talk about?' Laura paid for the broccoli which Brian handed her in a paper bag marked 'recycled'. Laura added the broccoli to other purchases in a large basket with leather handles somebody had brought her from Minorca. 'You get the authentic taste from Brian's veg,' she said. 'He's been seen scattering the contents of his cesspit over his patch when short of horse shit and his girlfriend, Susie, famous for her skin, quaffs her own urine every morning. She doesn't look more than thirteen; how's that for advertising organically grown food and back to nature?'

Claud followed Laura through the market. 'D'you remember my name?' he asked hopefully. It would be nice to get off the subject of Brian and back to himself.

'By association. Lifts? Elevators? Something like that?'

'Elevators?' Claud was at a loss. 'Lifts?'

'Miss Otis regrets – is Otis your real name?'

'My name is Claud Bannister,' said Claud offended.

Laura laughed. 'So it is. I wonder what made me think it was Otis? Got it, you are a writer.' She stressed the word, pinning it down. 'Banisters, stairs, not lifts.'

'You remember that.'

'How could I not? You had me trapped in a corner.

Undiscovered, but not disheartened, you said.'

'Was I so boring?' Claud's voice rose on a note of pain. 'I was going to suggest – to offer you a coffee, but if I—'

'Not boring at all. Yes, I'd love some coffee. It's draughty in this market, much as I enjoy it. Shall we go to the wine bar? The coffee is tolerable there.' Laura threaded her way through the stalls. Claud followed. 'As I remember it, you are writing a novel, have neither publisher nor money, but are determined to succeed. Right?'

'Oh yes, yes I am.'

'Why don't you keep a stall in the market?'

Entering the wine bar, Laura unwound her magenta-coloured scarf and unbuttoned her overcoat. She put them on a chair, her shopping basket on another and sat, effectively claiming for herself and Claud a table intended for four people.

Claud sat opposite her and after a moment's hesitation added his anorak to Laura's coat. 'What would I do with a stall?' he asked.

'Survive,' said Laura, 'while you write your books. I take it you are on unemployment benefit?'

'Lord, yes, but I'd lose it if I was caught running a stall. I wouldn't know how, anyway, and what would I sell?'

'Any sort of rubbish. Antiques? Old clothes? Old bottles from tips, your mother's cast-offs. It would pay better than the dole and keep you rich in ideas. You get a cross-section of people in the market.' Laura looked through the window of the wine bar which, steaming up, distorted the figures of people passing outside. Catching the eye of a man looking in, she raised a finger and mouthed, 'Hi.'

'Who was that?' asked Claud suspiciously.

'No idea. Just someone who thinks he knows me. What about an Irish coffee, it's cold enough?'

'Oh I—' (She knew the man, who was he?)

'I'll treat you. Maeve,' Laura caught a passing waitress by the skirt, 'two Irish coffees, please.'

'Okay,' said the girl, snatching away her skirt. 'No need to grab.'

Laura put a hand up to loosen the neck of her jersey. 'Lovely and warm in here, isn't it?' She looked about at the people coming in from the street; tables were filling up, but nobody challenged her right to the table for four.

'I was awfully pleased to meet you properly last night,' said Claud. 'I watched you. I wanted to get to know you the moment I saw you.'

'Oh?' Laura felt she must pay attention.

'You are so – er – colourful, nobody could fail to notice you.' Indeed in her orange skirt, black high-necked sweater and Cossack hat Laura was striking. Claud leaned towards her.

The waitress stretched across the table from behind Claud to place a mug of coffee laced with whiskey in front of Laura. Her bare arm brushed Claud's nose; he could smell her flesh, quite separate from the coffee; he jerked his head back as she set a second mug in front of him. 'Croissants,' she asked, 'or rolls?'

'Have some croissants,' suggested Laura. 'I shall.'

'Oh, thanks. Wonderful.' Claud, realising that he was hungry, salivated.

'Butter? Cherry jam?' enquired the waitress.

'Yes, please,' said Laura. 'You had got as far as colourful. That's a bit better than sidelong—'

'Oh, I, ah—' Claud was undecided. 'Er—'

'I love hearing about myself.' Laura sipped her coffee.

Claud watched her lips pout towards the mug. He liked the sharpness of her nose, her high cheek bones, extraordinarily bright eyes. 'The whites of your eyes are as brilliant as a child's,' he said.

'It's all the garlic I eat. Go on.'

'Your colouring is dramatic. Your - er - high colour, black hair and eyebrows, and the splendid colours you wear—'

The waitress, returning, thumped a plate of croissants, two tiny dishes of butter and two equally minuscule portions of jam onto the table.

'More, Maeve, more,' said Laura, without distracting her gaze from Claud.

'I have switched back to Mavis,' said the waitress. 'I am sick of the Irish shooting each other all the time. I disassociate myself from that tragic country; the Welsh are more reliable and harmonious.'

'Okay, Mavis, I'll try and remember,' said Laura. 'It's all the same to me. I happen to know you were born in Plymouth. Have you a manuscript one could look at?' She darted bright eyes at Claud.

Claud made a protective gesture, hands against chest.

'You will have to learn to accept criticism,' Laura grinned. 'You can't be pregnant for ever; somebody has to look at your baby.'

'My mother almost did; she was trying to tidy my room.'

'Tut! Still living at home?' Laura frowned.

'It saves money,' said Claud, abashed but unrepentant. He had invited Laura's nosiness, he told himself.

'If you keep a stall in the market, you will be able to afford digs. Maeve's mother, sorry, *Mavis*' mother has a spare room, I happen to know. A cosy sort of loft.' Laura gulped the coffee, which invigorated and exhilarated her. Buttering her croissant, she remembered that she had skipped breakfast. This would account for her elevation of spirit; it could not at her mature age be due to Claud's appearance. 'How old are you, baby?' she asked, her mouth full of croissant.

'What?' Claud's coffee nearly went the wrong way.

'I said, how old is your baby?' Laura emended.

'Oh, I see. Two paragraphs and sixteen sentences, to be exact.'

Claud sucked in his breath. Too late now to confess the true size of his manuscript, an unwieldy pile of much corrected typescript which haunted his nights and plagued his days. It contained, he realised as he looked at Laura, a mass of half-digested ideas, poor jokes, unresolved situations, phony descriptions of love-making and long descriptive passages in no way relative to the plot. What plot? Nervously he repeated, 'Two paragraphs and sixteen sentences.'

Laura was amused. They laughed. Claud felt immensely relieved. He was saved the risk of showing her his writing; he guessed she would despise it; he would jettison the bulk of it, start afresh.

Laura took off her hat and tossed back thick, springy hair.

'D'you want your bill?' asked Mavis, hovering.

'Not yet, thanks,' said Laura. 'I did ask for more butter and jam, Mavis. Is that loft of your mother's still to let?'

'Yes, she's upping the rent. There are people who want your table,' muttered Mavis.

'Then want must be their master; I get claustrophobia if squashed. I'll bring Claud round to see it. Do bring us our butter, Mavis.'

'Those people—'

'Perhaps they hope to share with us?' Laura looked dangerously round. 'Who are they?'

Three people waiting nearby moved away and squeezed themselves round a table for two, much cluttered with used cups, buttery plates and cigarette stubs squashed into saucers.

Laura munched her croissant and watched Mavis clear the table of its detritus, give it a perfunctory swish with a cloth and take the people's order. 'Mavis is an actress. She doesn't go on the dole, she takes this mean job and from this lowly position she observes human nature. She will weave all our mannerisms into her future parts. I shudder to think how I am contributing to some future box office draw. Perhaps you'd rather write plays?'

'No, thank you, that's not my line at all.' Claud shuddered at the thought.

'Well, at least you know that.'

'That's not a very kind thing to say, not in that tone of voice.'

'Who said I was kind? You accosted me, if I remember rightly. But never mind, I will fix you up with Mavis' mum and help you with your market stall.'

Claud gulped his coffee. The whiskey in it went ballooning into his brain. Laura had settled his future; he saw himself with a market stall. 'As long as I don't have to sell fish,' he said. 'I can't stand fish. I could work in a loft, though.'

'Right, then. All fixed. Jolly good,' said Laura. 'That bloody Mavis never brought our butter.'

'Keeping these chairs warm for us?' asked Brian Walker, coming in from the cold. 'Jolly good of you, Laura.' He began dismantling layers of outer clothing with one hand, while with the other he deftly hitched Laura's coat and Claud's anorak onto pegs near the door. 'Sit down there, sweet Susie,' he said to a tiny pink-nosed girl who had come in behind him. 'We've come for a plonk and pizza before going home. It's a ball-freezer behind that stall. This is my wife, Susie,' he said to Claud. 'Let her squeeze in beside you while I fetch us some grub. No use waiting for Maeve, she takes forever.'

'She's switched back to Mavis,' said Laura, amused. 'I seem to remember hearing she was plain Molly when she was at school. I was telling Claud about your lovely skin, Susie, but now he can see it for himself. Just look at her skin, Claud, isn't it perfect?'

'She tells everyone I wash in my pee,' said Susie, wiping her nose with the back of her hand. 'Have you got a handkerchief, Laura? Brian's pinched mine. He won't let me use tissues, it's all "Save the Trees" these days.'

'Use this,' said Laura, handing her a paper napkin. 'I'm told you drink it.'

Susie laughed. 'You terror.'

Brian returned, balancing pizzas and glasses of wine in enormous earthy hands. 'Here, treasure, get stuck into that.' He sat beside Susie, dwarfing her with his bulk.

Susie bit into her pizza with teeth in proportion to her size and sighed with pleasure. 'God, I was cold,' she said.

'Claud is going to keep a stall in the market and lodge with Mavis' mum so that he can write his novels,' said Laura.

'Laura's a great fixer of other people's problems,' said Brian. 'What shall you sell from your stall?'

'Antiques,' said Claud, answering for himself. 'Junk.' He was beginning to visualise an agreeable future with a stall in the market close to Brian and

Susie, who really did have the most incredible skin, pale and pinkly glowing, as fresh as a small child's. Could one believe?

Laura wrote on the back of an envelope. 'That's Mavis' mum's address,' she said. 'She's called Mrs Kennedy. Let me know how you get on. Bye, Susie, bye, Brian.' She slithered into her coat, swung the magenta scarf around her neck, held it across her face so that they could only see her eyes, and crammed the Cossack hat onto her head, tipping it low over her forehead. 'See you—' And she was gone.

'But—' Claud clutched the envelope, watched Laura's departing back. 'She promised to take me there, to introduce me, to—'

'She's written the scenario, you act it,' said Susie, 'she's like that. She's not going to fix the rent for you.'

'I never supposed—' began Claud, who had supposed exactly that. 'I don't understand.'

'You are not meant to,' said Brian. 'What's this butter for, Mavis?'

'Laura asked for it,' said Mavis, standing gracefully near the table.

'Will she pay for it?' asked Brian.

'Oh, yes.'

'Okay, we will eat it. She seems also to have left us a croissant.' He split the croissant and shared it with Susie. 'Have another coffee?' he suggested to Claud.

'Thanks very much, that would be nice.' Claud sat back. He had been in half a mind to run after Laura, make a date to be taken to see Mrs Kennedy's loft or at least arrange another meeting.

'Irish?' enquired Mavis, gaining his attention; she looked bored, as though she was chewing gum, which she was not.

'Welsh,' said Claud, banishing her boredom. 'Is she

always like that?' he reverted to Laura. 'She left rather suddenly. I thought she - er—'

'When we warm up we smell of dung,' said Brian. 'It offends Laura's delicate nose.'

Susie snuffled with laughter into her glass of wine.

Claud was uncertain whether Brian was serious; he felt it would be offensive on such a short acquaintance to sniff, yet Brian did look very earthy, his fingernails rimmed in brown, his green wellies streaked with what might easily be manure. Mavis put another mug of coffee in front of him. 'Oh,' said Claud, 'oh dear! She went off without - oh - I must - oh.' He clapped a hand to his breast pocket.

'That's okay,' said Mavis, standing very close. 'She keeps an account here. I'm off soon,' she said. 'I'll take you home to see my mother if you are really interested in the loft. Have you finished, Brian and Susie? Because if you have I want to clear the table.'

'How brutal you are,' said Susie, refusing to be rushed. 'They don't employ you here to harass us customers.'

'They don't know that I do,' said Mavis, gathering plates and cups onto a tray. 'Come on, have a heart. I want to get home and wash my hair.'

'Have you noticed Mavis' hair?' asked Brian, keeping a tight hold of his wine glass. 'It really is that colour, she doesn't do anything to it.'

'Tangerine,' said Susie. 'And her eyes are jade, her teeth like little chips of Carrara marble.' She nudged Claud. 'You hadn't noticed how delicious she is, had you?'

'He was taken up with Laura,' said Brian. 'Can I pay next week, Mavis dear?'

'Certainly not,' said Mavis, snatching Brian's glass

and clunking it onto her tray. 'Only Laura has a special arrangement, you know that.'

'Oh, all right, you great bully.' Brian reached for his coat, handed Susie hers. 'This should cover it.' He gave Mavis a ten pound note. 'Keep the change.'

'I'm not proud,' said Mavis, laughing. 'I won't be a minute,' she said to Claud, 'if you care to wait.'

'I'll wait,' said Claud, 'thanks.' My goodness, he thought, she is pretty; how could I not have noticed?

Brian was buttoning Susie into her jacket as though she was a small child. 'Where's your woolly hat?' he asked.

Claud watched them, amused. He felt elated at meeting these new people, Laura's friends.

'In your pocket.' Susie let herself be dressed by Brian, who now put a wool cap on her head. 'Laura wouldn't let you do this to her,' she remarked, sitting doll-like.

'Laura would not let me get a leg over her, either,' said Brian.

'I wouldn't let you try,' said Susie amiably. 'Not over anyone and particularly not over Laura.'

'All the same, one wonders what motivates her.' Brian gently pushed tendrils of Susie's hair up under her cap with a large forefinger, then leaned forward and kissed her mouth.

'Sex?' suggested Susie, returning the kiss.

'Who with?' asked Claud, watching them.

'One doesn't know,' said Brian.

'There are lots of stories,' said Susie.

'Nothing you can pin down,' said Brian.

'Is she married?' asked Claud. 'Or was she, ever?'

'That's one thing that is known: she's not nor ever was.'

'Does one know why not?' Claud persisted. He felt a need to know, was there some sadness? 'Did some bloke betray her?'

'That's a mystery, but any betraying to be done would have been done by Laura.' Susie surprised him by her cattiness.

Claud felt angry with Susie. Laura had left them so suddenly, she had made herself defenceless. Unequal to the task on such short acquaintance, he was grateful to Mavis who, rejoining them, had overheard Susie's remarks.

'You may be wrong there,' said Mavis. 'My mum has a theory that Laura wouldn't hurt a fly.'

Claud recollected his own parent the evening before suggesting a heart of nougat.

Brian said, 'An older woman, out of the race, would be a better judge than you, Susie.'

'Perhaps she is just self-sufficient,' suggested Mavis. 'It's not absolutely necessary, as you men seem to think, for every girl to have a man,' she added tartly.

'Just nicer,' said Susie, getting to her feet.

'See you in the market when you've got your stall,' said Susie, now ready to leave. 'Brian and I will show you anything Laura forgets to tell you. Bye.'

'Goodbye, see yer,' said Brian. 'Come on, sugar.' He pushed Susie out ahead of him.

'Brrr,' exclaimed Susie, gasping in the frosty air. 'Icicles!'

'Are they really married?' Claud asked Mavis, who stood now beside him, buttoned into an overcoat several sizes too large.

'Common law,' said Mavis. 'Come on.'

* * *

Laura, rising from the dentist's chair in the surgery across the street where she had been having her teeth scaled and polished, watched Claud take Mavis' arm as they stepped out of the wine bar. 'You certainly see local life from your window, Mr Owen.'

'I haven't time,' said the dentist, 'or the inclination. See you again in six months, Miss Thornby. Next,' he said into the intercom.

'You miss a lot,' said Laura, ignoring his rudeness.

'Ah, well.' He was impatient to see her go.

And what am I missing? Laura speculated as she descended the stairs. What have I missed, she questioned as she wrapped her coat round her against the cold wind, swung her scarf round her neck as she stood on the dentist's doorstep. Far down the street she could see Claud's fair head lean towards Mavis' orange aureole as they broke into a trot to avoid an oncoming car. She turned to walk in the opposite direction, lengthening her stride. I wonder why he is against fish. What would Freud say? More to the point, what do I say? She smiled as she thought that there was really no need for her to miss anything.

Brian and Susie, passing her in their battered old Land-Rover waved, assuming that Laura's smile was for them.

'Found yourself a toy boy?'

Laura, turning, stood nose to nose with Nicholas Thornby who, softly shod, had crept up behind her.

'Looking at you, dear Nicholas,' she answered at a tangent, 'I can see what I shall look like when I am really old.' She stepped back a pace to observe him better. 'A trim figure, not too wrinkled but pretty thin on top,' she said, amused that he should bother to jerk his stomach in for her, a reflex action.

'You'll be so lucky, your mother and I are uniquely preserved. But who is the boy? He's pretty,' Nicholas persisted.

'Claud Bannister.'

'Margaret Bannister's boy? He used to be so spotty, I didn't recognise him.'

'Ever beautiful, you must have had your share of acne in your day? I know I did.'

'It's too far back to remember. Why are you taking him up? I saw you with him in the market. You don't usually go for lame dogs.'

'Does he look lame?' Laura wrapped her scarf tighter against the icy wind. 'Rather than live on the dole, he's going to run a junk stall in the market,' she said.

'How laudable.' Nicholas' tone indicated doubt.

'I thought I'd offer him a look round the Old Rectory attics, it's high time some of the debris was cleared out.'

'You may have to ask Emily's and my permission.'

'I shall, perhaps.'

'I don't know what Emily will say.'

'She will ask if it's in a good cause and if it's not, she'll be glad of a clearance.'

'How well you know her.' Nicholas grinned. 'One questions whether a toy boy is a good cause.' Laura did not respond to this. 'But there may be treasures in that attic,' Nicholas prevaricated. 'One can't be too careful. Priceless Ming vases used as umbrella stands, one reads in the paper,' he said, laughing.

'That's not very likely.' It was Laura's turn to laugh. 'Quite a lot of stuff was put there by me, things the dustmen refused to move.'

'Oh those dustmen! Bone idle scroungers.'

Laura blinked her eyes, which were watering from the wind, and sniffed, twitching a nose that was a feminine version of Nicholas'. 'I know you vote Tory,' she said as she stepped aside to allow a woman pushing a double buggy to pass.

'One should not pander to the unemployed,' said Nicholas, stepping back close to her.

'So I have frequently heard you say. We are blocking the pavement,' said Laura.

'I also saw you chatting to him at the concert the other night.'

'I have an idea he once worked in a fish shop,' said Laura, sowing a red herring in Nicholas' mind.

'I thought you were interested in that Roumanian conductor (that was pretty trashy stuff, wasn't it?). Isn't it a bit of a comedown to switch to a fishmonger?'

'The Roumanian has gone back to Roumania.'

'A communist country, no joy there, I agree. One could see you weren't much interested but he wasn't lame, was he?'

'Not so that you'd notice.'

'And this Claud Bannister, shall you lame him?'

'The traffic warden has just stuck a ticket on the windscreen of your car, Nicholas.' A man in a tweed hat adorned with salmon flies tossed the information over his shoulder as he elbowed past Laura. 'While you stand there gassing like an old maid, blocking the way of legitimate shoppers, you get ticketed. Just wait till they bring clamps to the town!' His voice faded as he hurried out of earshot.

'Damn and blast, that's the third this month,' said Nicholas. 'Your fault for keeping me talking,' he said nastily.

Laura smiled. 'Too bad. Tough,' she said.

'He's a bit young for a toy boy,' Nicholas niggled.

'I heard he was a lift boy in some hotel.' Laura tried a fresh herring.

'What versatility! Those tight trousers and bum-freezer jackets. Not my style, alas. I would hardly think—'

'Nicholas,' said a tweedy lady burdened with shopping, 'that fiend of a warden has stuck a ticket on your—'

'I know, I know,' cried Nicholas, furiously. 'What's it got to do with you, you silly cow?' He began to move back down the street to his car.

Laura watched Nicholas go with detachment. Then she shouted after him, 'I'll treat you and Emily to a booze-up tonight, how about it? A pub crawl?'

Nicholas waved an arm in acknowledgement. Laura continued on her way, leaning slightly into the wind, protecting her face with her scarf, wondering why she felt protective towards Claud; he wouldn't thank me for the fishmonger or the lifts, she thought, but maybe he will when he's famous.

Christopher Peel, sitting beside his wife Helen driving their BMW, noticed Laura as she parted from Nicholas. Craning his neck the better to look back, he reflected not for the first time that there were compensations in having a wife who did not trust one's driving. One could see what was going on without being accused of risking an accident.

'That's Laura in another garish outfit,' said Helen, who was suspected by some of having eyes in the back of her head. 'God knows why she wears such an outrageous combination of colours; somebody should tell her.'

'Why don't you tell her?' Losing sight of Laura as

Helen accelerated through the traffic, Christopher slewed his eyes towards his wife. A greater contrast than Helen's clothes with Laura's would be hard to find, he thought, appraising Helen's sensible sludge-coloured sweater and shirt, matching corduroy slacks, dull green waxed waterproof jacket with corduroy collar, brown felt hat. 'Sludge,' he said, assessing his wife's complexion (nothing worse than a fading suntan with mouse-coloured hair, he thought). 'Sludge.'

'What?' said Helen.

'Nothing.' (I bet she heard me.)

'I wonder what she is doing down here, she hardly ever visits Emily and Nicholas for more than a day,' said Helen.

'Oh, I don't know,' said Christopher, who knew quite well that Laura came down oftener than was generally known. 'Perhaps she feels responsible for the old people.'

'Responsible! Laura?' Helen snorted.

'Well—'

'She must be up to something if she's down for more than a day—'

'She's got her pad in the Old Rectory.'

'Is she having an affair with that red composer?'

'What red composer? I thought he was the conductor.' Christopher betrayed himself.

'Don't be dim, Christopher, the man who wrote that awful stuff we had to sit through at the charity concert; that man.'

'How would I know?' (Sitting in the wine bar with that boy. If she'd been on her own as she usually is, I would have gone in and asked her why the hell she—)

'She's an old flame of yours.'

'Not that again! Oh God, Helen, why can't you lay off? Any small flicker I may have had with Laura was twenty-five years ago.'

'More than that.'

'So you know it all. Why don't you tackle Laura yourself? Tell her you don't like her clothes, ask her who she is sleeping with, why she visits her mother, why—'

'No need to fly off the handle.' Helen changed gear.

'I am not flying—'

'You are so touchy about Laura.'

'It is you who are touchy about Laura, Helen, you never stop, you—'

'I never mention Laura. I just happened to notice her at the concert the other night and to make a small observation just now. No need to blow it up—'

'Christ, Helen, Laura and I were practically brought up together. We were childhood friends, she was constantly in our house, she—'

'She would have married you if your father hadn't put his foot down. I don't suppose your mother had a clue – so wrapped up in herself, her bloody dogs and her ridiculous garden.'

'Look, Helen.' Christopher raised his voice, shouting above the noise of a lorry Helen was overtaking. 'Laura never wanted to marry me, she—'

'Of course she did. Obviously she wanted your money and the house. God knows what *she* would have done with the garden if she'd got her hands on it.'

'She did *not* want to marry me!' Christopher shouted, and a hitherto somnolent old labrador raised its head from among the parcels and packages on the back seat and barked. 'When will you get it into your stupid head that there was never any question of marriage between Laura and me? The moment she was old enough, she upsticked and beat it to London. She made a career for herself, she has her own business—'

'A pretty small one—'

'– I don't see why you should be so upset and—'

'It's you who seem to be upset.' Helen paused by the traffic lights on the edge of the town.

'Oh, God,' said Christopher.

'Actually,' said Helen as the lights turned to green, 'if you hadn't flown into this silly temper, I was leading up to the fact that I have a small job—'

'For her small business?'

'Yes.'

'Then why—'

'I thought you could persuade her to do it for me at cost price or something.'

'I could?'

'Yes, you know her better than I, as you've just indicated.'

'So—'

'And *I* don't want to know her better than I do already.'

'That makes two of you,' Christopher muttered. 'What's the job?' he asked. 'I don't see why she should do it at cost price, she has her living to make.'

'It was just a thought, since you are such old buddies.'

Disliking the word buddy Christopher thought, If I told Helen that if it were not for her I would seldom think of Laura, she wouldn't believe me. He watched the road ahead. Perhaps, he thought, I should be grateful to Helen. Glancing at his wife's profile he smiled, then patting her corduroy thigh he said loudly:

'You silly old thing, what's the job?'
Helen proceeded to tell him.

Laura, walking slowly in spite of the cold, watched Christopher and Helen's car disappear and thought, Poor old, boring old Christopher. She wrapped her scarf close, pushing it up over her jaw. She dawdled, looking into a bookshop window, keeping her eyes down, not wishing to enter into chat with the bookseller, who was in his way a friend. She counted the titles: love, crime, travel, history. By dawdling it was her intention to give Nicholas time to make a scene with the traffic warden, who was lurking within insult distance of Nicholas' car. Either the man had more courage than was good for him or he was new to the town. Only a few years ago Nicholas had tripped a warden so that, lurching against a bollard on the quay, he had fallen into the river. I cannot but admire, thought Laura, watching. The old devil does not resist his impulses; he has a dreadful, endearing, childlike quality.

Nicholas approached his car; the warden, taller and burlier than Nicholas, stood his ground (Laura asked herself which of the two men needed her protection). Nicholas snatched the ticket stuck behind his wiper and tore it across. Obeying an instinct similar to that of a dog confronted by a cat, its back arched, its mouth spitting, the warden shrugged and turned away.

Laura chuckled, ran her tongue over her freshly scaled teeth and, relaxing, let her thoughts return pleasurably to Claud, so fresh and ingenuous after Clug. He was vulnerable in a way Clug could never have been, more importantly so than Christopher in youth. I could protect Claud, she thought, then almost laughed outright as she was swept by an irresistible exultant desire to interfere, manipulate, experiment with Claud – by way of protection.

'You reach it up this thing. I'll go first.' Mavis climbed a metal ladder towards a trap-door in the ceiling. She still wore her greatcoat. Claud, watching her climb, resisted nipping her Achilles tendon between finger and thumb. 'A well turned ankle,' he said, reaching up but not touching.

'A what? Come on up.' She had disappeared.

'Dornford Yates or Somerset Maugham, perhaps?' Claud climbed the ladder.

Above him Mavis switched on a light. 'It's pretty basic,' she said as he came up through the floor, 'just the bed, a table, a chair, the bookshelves. You'll need somewhere to keep your clothes.'

The loft was larger than he had expected; cold light streamed through attic windows. Claud went to the window. 'Oh,' he said, 'what a view!'

'Yes,' said Mavis, 'yes.' She stuffed her hands up the sleeves of her coat.

They looked across slate roofs and jumbled chimney pots to the town gasworks, and to the right the river, where boats moored in midstream, swans and ducks cruised. The air in the attic was dry. Claud sneezed and, when he breathed in again, sniffed the faint smell he had noticed when, reaching across the table in the wine bar, Mavis had set the coffee in front of Laura. Fresh flesh. He felt simultaneously a wish to kiss Mavis' throat as it emerged from the heavy coat and something which resembled lust for Laura. Watching the gasometer, he sighed as the twin desires cancelled each other out.

Hearing the sigh, Mavis questioned, 'So it won't do? As I said, it's pretty basic.' She excused the loft. 'It's not even an attic.'

'No, no, it's lovely. I could bring some rugs from home. Do you think your mother will rent it to me? What's the rent?'

'Let's go and ask her.' Mavis led the way down the ladder. She feared her mother would find the prospective tenant too young; she wanted a steady tenant who would not be likely to negotiate the ladder drunk. There had been an unfortunate incident with a visiting cousin who had slipped and been badly bruised. Since this episode Ann Kennedy had dreaded an entanglement with insurance companies. On the other hand a tenant of guaranteed sobriety might not be sufficiently spry to negotiate the ladder. It was a worry; she needed the rent. 'Don't be surprised if you hear me tell my mother that you don't drink,' said Mavis.

'I don't, much. I can't afford to. Why?' Claud rejoined Mavis at the foot of the ladder.

'She's afraid of people falling off the ladder pissed.'

'I'm pretty good on ladders, drunk or sober,' said Claud primly.

'It's the Irish imagination which foresees possible trouble.'

'I thought you were a Plymouth family,' said Claud, watching the back of Mavis' head as she descended the stairs ahead of him.

'So what? There are Kennedys born all over. In the United States, for instance. You've been listening to Laura.' Mavis, not over-fond of Laura, sounded quite huffy.

'I suppose everyone tells you you have beautiful

hair?' Claud attempted to deflect her huff.

'They certainly do.' Mavis was unenthusiastic. Then, remembering her mother's need for the rent, she said, 'Come on and meet my mum. Mum,' she shouted, 'where are you?'

'In here,' Ann Kennedy answered from the kitchen.

'This is Claud, a friend of Laura's, he'd like to rent the loft, Mum.'

'Rent the loft?' said Ann Kennedy, affecting surprise. 'A friend of Laura's? Well!' Impossible to tell from her tone whether Mrs Kennedy thought well or ill of Laura. 'I'm defrosting the fridge; it's a job which bores me rigid.' She waved towards an open refrigerator. 'Takes forever.'

'Soften it up with the hairdrier,' suggested Mavis.

'Would that be safe?' Mrs Kennedy was interested. 'Wouldn't I get electrocuted?'

'It's a lovely loft.' Claud hastened to stem the diversion. Suddenly he wanted the loft badly; he could see his typewriter on the table, hear his fingers tap the keys. 'I am a writer, Mrs Kennedy.'

'A writer,' said Ann Kennedy in flat tone. 'Oh.' She bent to peer into the fridge. 'It is beginning to drip, perhaps the drier – this fridge is as old as Methuselah.'

'I am very quiet,' said Claud in recommendation.

'Quiet,' said Ann Kennedy. 'Really?'

'Yes,' said Claud.

'There's the ladder.'

'I'm pretty nimble.'

'I don't doubt.'

'I scarcely drink.'

'Scarcely.'

'I could pay the rent in advance, if it's not too large, that is.'

'M-m-m.' She peered into the refrigerator.

'Cash,' said Claud.

'Cash,' said Mrs Kennedy. 'Did you tell him the rent, Maeve?'

'*Mavis*,' said Mavis. 'No, I didn't.'

'If you must keep changing your name,' said Ann Kennedy in accents of extreme irritability, 'why can't you choose one we can all stick to? A decent biblical name like Ruth or Rebecca or Miriam?' Her voice rose as ice suddenly began to clatter noisily onto the ice tray. 'Or Mary? What's wrong with the virgin Mary?'

'It's common.'

'There's only one virgin Mary,' snapped Ann Kennedy, 'why not—'

'Because I can't stand the Jews forever killing the Arabs and vice versa, they are as bad as the Northern Irish.' Mavis' voice rose to meet her parent's.

'It would be simpler with all this chopping and changing to know you by a number. Number One would suit you fine,' Ann Kennedy snapped.

Claud registered that this was a well-established conflict. 'Could we get back to the rent?' His masculine calm rather pleased him.

'Of course.' Mrs Kennedy stooped to field an oblong wedge of ice which was slipping towards the floor. 'Gotcher.' She named a rent high in excess of the amount he had expected. 'Any friend of Laura's is welcome.' She avoided her daughter's eye.

'Great,' said Claud. 'Perhaps I could move in next week?'

The telephone shrilled in the next room. Before answering Claud's question Ann Kennedy moved away to answer it. Waiting for her to return, Claud watched Mavis standing dwarfed in her immense coat, her face a mixture of surprise and something else. 'What's the matter?' he asked, feeling that if he were to become a writer, he must be sensitive to people's moods.

'Nothing,' said Mavis, torn between admiration for her mother's bold greed and fear that on reflection Claud might change his mind.

'That was Laura,' said Ann Kennedy, returning.

'Oh?'

'Message for you to ring her up or go and see her.'

'Me?' asked Mavis.

'No. Mr – er – what's your name?'

'Claud Bannister.'

'That's right, Claud. I'm glad she rang. I was a bit bothered about the rent.' Mrs Kennedy bent to catch another bit of ice effecting its escape. 'So I asked her; she said knock off a couple of quid.' Mother's and daughter's eyes met.

'No business of Laura's,' said Mavis.

'I'm quite happy with what you—' began Claud.

'No, no. As I say, knock off two pounds. She said either give her a tinkle or come over, she could tell you something about your stall. You didn't say anything about a stall?'

'Well, no. No, I didn't. I could go over this afternoon. Thanks. Would you come with me, Mavis? Show me the way?'

'I have to wash my hair,' said Mavis. 'You'll find it all right.' She pulled her coat collar up over her chin. Claud was reminded of Laura wrapping her scarf across her face in the wine bar. She had looked exotic. Mavis disappearing into the outsize overcoat gave the effect of a tortoise. 'There's a bus,' said Mavis, 'catch that.'

* * *

Arriving at the Old Rectory, Claud was not in the best of tempers. He had consulted the timetable but arrived to see the bus leaving the square minutes earlier than he expected. On protesting to a youth waiting for a bus in the opposite direction, he had been outraged at the suggestion that he had studied the wrong timetable. 'It's winter, zee, you should look for winter times not zummer times.' The boy leaned against the wall, grinning. 'Ain't no more buzzes 'til zix thirty or so.' Humiliated by the fake yokel accent and the suspicion that he had in fact made a stupid mistake, Claud set off walking, more with the intention of distancing himself from mockery than of reaching Laura.

As he walked annoyance coupled with his imagination spurred him along. Not profligate with ideas, he would use the incident in his new novel: his hero, as yet rather an intangible character, would foot it towards the girl he loved. Naturally he would have to walk somewhere more inspiring than this main road with its draggle of bungaloid habitations punctuated by filling stations. He would set him to walk over a moor, across the Fens or along the Pennine Way, somewhere more peaceable than a main road where cars hurtled past breaking the speed limit, polluting the air with disgusting fumes; he would walk towards his lover, waiting expectantly.

Passing the last filling station, Claud consoled himself for this boring trudge by giving his hero a bicycle, then, growing impatient with the tedious journey, he bought him a car. It was hard to decide on the make. He was snobbish about Fords, averse to Fiats and despised Sunbeams, but by the time he read on a white board half-hidden in a laurel hedge the words, 'The Old Rectory', he had bought his hero a second-hand Alfa Romeo. With that little matter settled he could apply himself to his character's destiny in the next chapter.

Claud walked up a curving drive to the front door and rang the bell.

A dog barked loudly. The door burst open. Laura, twenty years older than she had been that morning, beckoned him in. 'Come in, come in, are you in trouble? Run out of petrol? Car broken down? Want to use the telephone?' She backed into a dark hall. 'Or have you come to read the meters?'

'I walked - I—'

'Walked! Heavens! Nobody walks. The road is lethal. I am surprised you were not squashed like a hedgehog. I'll show you the meter, you're new—'

'Laura - I - you—'

'Oh! You want *Laura*,' said Laura's double. 'Round the back, try that, servants' entrance.'

'Oh - I'm sorry, I mistook, I thought - I—'

'Round the house, the other door.' The door so brusquely opened clicked shut in his face.

Repulsed, Claud made his way along an alley which led through overgrown shrubs to a door at the back of the house. There was a knocker. Claud knocked.

'I can see by your face that you met my mother,' said Laura, opening the door. 'She gets tremendously annoyed if she's mistaken for me, which is a pity because I had an idea that we might prise some junk for your stall out of her; the attic is bulging with tat. Come in.'

Claud followed her along an ill-lit passage into a combination of kitchen and sitting-room. Where once a kitchen range had stood was a large open fire, along one wall a gas cooker, sink and refrigerator, in front of the fire a shabby sofa and armchairs. Behind the sofa stood a long deal table, one end obviously used to eat off, the other to work at. A dresser held books as well as china. The room was warm and smelled agreeably of garlicky cooking but beneath this aroma there was a hint of mice. The view from the windows was on to a large neglected garden. Claud felt his spirits rise. 'Nice,' he said, 'it's nice.'

'Well - yes - it does. I've walled them off.'

'Who?'

'Family.'

'Oh.'

'I sleep in what was the servants' hall, and my bathroom was the pantry. I'm not here much.'

'I got your message.'

'I gathered from Mrs K that you've rented the loft. Sit down, do.' She pointed to an armchair occupied by a cat.

Claud sat, edging next to the cat, held his hands towards the fire. 'Yes I have, it's superb.'

'I used to rent it myself,' said Laura. 'I put the bed and table there, and the chair.'

'Really?' Claud was surprised. 'What for?'

'Privacy. To escape. I spent my pocket money on it. I lay and dreamed and counted my pimples.'

'Oh.'

'You know what it's like when family become oppressive, unbearable.'

'Well, actually, I—' Claud thought of his gentle unobtrusive mother. 'Not exactly, my—'

'Drink? Tea? Coffee? Wine? Did you walk?'

'Yes, your mother seemed surprised. Coffee, please.'

'Walking, the lost art.' Laura poured beans into a grinder and filled the room with its screech. 'Sorry about that, it's French,' she excused the grinder. She switched on an electric kettle. 'No one in their right senses walks along that road, you should have come over the hill across the fields, or come by bus.'

'I missed it.'

'People do.' Laura poured boiling water onto the coffee, stirred the mix in a jug. Claud, breathing its heavenly smell, found himself telling Laura about his hero who, starting out as a pedestrian, was now the owner of an Alfa Romeo.

'How splendidly vulgar.' Laura peered into the coffee jug. 'Nearly ready. What's his name, your hero?'

'Justin.'

'Oh God!' said Laura. 'You can't call him Justin.'

'Why ever not?' Claud was nettled.

'You just cannot.' Laura poured coffee through a strainer into beautiful but chipped cups and handed one to Claud. 'Milk? Sugar? Help yourself. I've got a cake somewhere.' She moved to the dresser, where a half-demolished cake sagged crumbling on a broken Worcester plate. 'Justin,' she said, 'is *un*splendidly vulgar.'

'Um.' Claud gulped his coffee. It burned. He could feel the burn right down into his chest. 'I'll have to think about that.' He was not prepared to yield, knew that he would and must take care not to tell Laura that the choice of name had hovered between Justin and Crispin.

Laura subsided in a flowing movement to sit cross-legged in front of the fire; she had taken off her boots and was now barefoot.

'You have beautiful feet,' said Claud.

'Yes.' Laura tucked them out of sight under her skirt. 'I know.'

'I thought your mother was your *doppelgänger*,' said Claud.

'And well she might be,' said Laura. 'There's a male version too.' She did not explain. 'Have you seduced Mavis yet?' she asked.

'I haven't had time,' said Claud. Two can play at this, he thought, watching Laura's face in the firelight; what does she take me for?

Laura showed her teeth; she had her back to the light and might have been smiling, it was difficult to tell. 'Have some cake.' She proffered the plate. 'That's not mouse shit, it's seed cake,' she said as Claud hesitated.

'No thanks.' He recoiled.

'Well,' said Laura, 'since you are here we'd better brave the *doppelgängers*.' She reached for a pair of tights hanging on the fireguard and began putting them on.

Claud observed her legs; they were long and peculiarly neat. Her movements as she pulled the tights up over her bottom had a sensuality which brought the word *risqué* to what he was beginning to think of as his writer's mind. 'I would like to seduce *you*,' he said. He decided to give his heroine Laura's body. She had already, he realised, got Mavis' hair in his writer's mind's eye. He had become aware of Mavis and the smell of her flesh in the wine bar, but he had been taken up with Laura, and later all he had seen of her was the enormous overcoat; she had even hidden her hands in its sleeves. 'I would like to seduce you,' he repeated.

'Fancy that,' said Laura, picking up the telephone and dialling. 'I am coming round,' she said as someone answered, 'to explore the attic.' Then, 'You'd put in a bit of practice before tackling Mavis, would that be it?'

Claud did not know what to make of this.'I don't

know what to make of you,' he said. Surely at this juncture any woman of Laura's age would laugh and say, I am old enough to be your mother, or words to that effect.

But Laura gave him what that morning he had called her sidelong look. 'Just concentrate on Justin,' she said. 'And what is his lover's name to be?'

'I haven't decided yet.' Quickly he dismissed the name he had been toying with, it would never do. Pearl must be dropped back where it came from. Indeed later when he tried to remember the name he could not and even believed it might have been Fleur, or perhaps June.

Laura tugged at her boots. 'Coming?' she asked.

With his back to the light Claud poured tea from the pot his mother had placed before him. His eye was extremely painful, his head throbbed. Beside the teapot his mother had put a bottle of aspirin. The scene revived memories of the times before his father left home, driven away by his wife's intolerable forbearance.

Claud unscrewed the aspirin bottle, tipped pills onto his palm, gulped them down with scalding tea, drained the cup and refilled it. My pa, he thought, was an incurable alcoholic; he did not last long after leaving Ma's tender care. Perhaps if they could have had a hearty row, a healthy shout when he came home drunk, he would be alive to this day? But *I* was not roaring drunk last night, Claud told himself. I am not an alcoholic. On the other hand recollection of what happened in the Old Rectory is dim, if not zero. 'I think I got a bang on the head,' he said as his mother rustled the sheets of her newspaper. 'I probably have a slight concussion.'

Margaret Bannister, an inveterate *Guardian* reader, did not answer. Claud calculated that she had just about reached the leader page after starting at the back with the sports; she was unlikely to reply to his remark until she had worked through to the front page. By that time the aspirin and tea would have begun their work. Thinking this, Claud realised what he had not realised before: that this ploy had evolved over years of his father's hangovers. (Make strong tea, supply aspirin, give it time to work before speaking.)

But what had happened at the Old Rectory? Claud cudgelled his brain. He had followed Laura round the house and in at the door where he had earlier been rebuffed by her mother. On the way Laura had said something he did not quite catch about 'disturbing my haunts'; it did not make sense and she had not repeated it. She had pushed open the door, paused in the hall and listened. This in itself seemed odd at the time; any normal daughter entering her mother's house would call out, 'I'm here,' or, 'Anyone at home?' or words to that effect. But Laura put finger to lip, signalled him to follow and then walked fast and quietly along the hall and up the stairs. He had followed her up and along a landing, through a green baize door and up a steep, uncarpeted flight to the attic. Here Laura stopped looking puzzled and pushed open a door, motioning him to follow. He remembered getting the impression that she had expected the door to be shut.

It was while Laura fumbled for a light switch – 'Wait there, you might fall over something' – that it had happened.

A bucket was clapped over his head. There was a rat-tat-tat of blows on its outside. The noise was terrifying. He remembered stepping back, falling down the stairs, bumping and banging his head, his nose and his eye as he rolled, tearing off the bucket and scrambling to his feet. Above in the dark of the attic there was the sound of scuffling, grunts, gasps, hisses. It was the absence of voices he had found unnerving. Making no effort to help Laura, he had taken to his heels and fled. As he left the house he heard a burst of laughter.

Sitting in his mother's warm kitchen gulping tea, swilling down the aspirin, Claud felt shame for his pusillanimity as he remembered running down the drive to the road, thumbing a lift from a passing van, being dropped off at a public house. He had sat in the pub trembling with shock (it must have been shock, not fear). At some moment during the evening's drinking (yes, now he remembered drinking. Quite a lot, actually) Brian and Susie had joined him. Yes, that's right, they had talked about his future in the market and given him a lift home. Once inside the door he had vomited. It can't have been very late because his mother had still been up and about. She hadn't said anything. She had watched him clear up his sick; he had been well enough to do that. She had said nothing, absolutely nothing; no wonder his father left home. Claud felt a comradely wave of sympathy for his father, who he usually referred to as 'a perfect shit', 'a prize shit', 'a wimp'. Reviving under the influence of the strong tea and aspirin, Claud felt rage and remembered his fury of the night before. He had made a long abrasive speech to his mother before staggering upstairs to bed, the last few steps on all fours. What the hell had he *said*?

Margaret Bannister folded her newspaper and sat down. She had, while reading the newspaper, put butter and marmalade on the table and also made toast. This feminine gift of doing several things at once without being flustered had maddened his father. (Why can't you concentrate on one thing at a time? Have you got three arms, woman?)

'Your education is going to waste.' Margaret spoke in derisory quotes. She buttered her toast; the scraping sound jarred on Claud's delicate ear. Normally about as fierce as a lettuce, she sounded jaunty and crisp as she repeated the phrase, 'Your education is going to waste,' before biting her toast.

Assuming attack to be the best form of defence, Claud snarled, 'Mother, you are whining. Why don't you go the whole hog, come straight out, cast your sacrifices in my teeth? No new clothes, no holidays, no decent car, long years of pinching and scraping.' Let her whine. Surely she would whine? What if he had come in drunk and been sick in the hall; he had cleared it up, hadn't he? 'I am not going to take those exams again.' He raised his voice. 'I do not want to become an accountant.'

'That idea for a career was entirely your choice, as I remember. Pass the marmalade.'

Claud lumbered on: 'I am going to be a writer and support myself until I get published by keeping a stall in the market.'

'So you said last night. Toast?'

'Did I?'

'Yes.' Margaret Bannister put more bread into the toaster. 'You did.'

Keeping in profile, so that she would not get a good look at his battered eye, Claud squinted at his parent. 'Did I say all that?'

'Not quite so clearly; your speech was on the slur.' His mother caught the toast as it sprang from the toaster, putting one piece in the toast rack, which she nudged towards her son, the other on her plate.

Claud ploughed on. 'You can look the other way when you go marketing.' He had often raised a laugh among friends at university by describing his mother as 'poor but snobbish'. He had even sung, 'She was poor, but she was snobbish' to the music hall aria after a drink or two. 'I am moving out of here.' He raised his voice. 'I have rented Mrs Kennedy's loft.'

Rarely since adolescence had he been so disagreeable to his mother. Why did she not whine? If only she would whine, he would feel less awful, less like his father. There would be the justification to sprint upstairs and pack his bags (he would have to come back for his books and the heavier things).

'You told me that last night.' Good God, she was laughing! 'Ha, ha, ha, hah!' Helpless laughter! Tears of laughter. 'Oh, Claud, if you could see yourself!' She wiped her eyes. 'Oh, it hurts to laugh so much, oh!' Her laughter bubbled again. 'It was your choice to be an accountant. You wanted security. Security!' Mrs Bannister hiccuped with mirth. 'We never were secure in my family, never went in for accountants, and certainly not in your father's. Now there's snobbery for you.'

Good God, she must know, must have heard me. 'Perhaps I am rebelling against your joint fecklessness,' he mumbled, confidence crumbling.

'I think your plan excellent; a stall in the market could be a lot of fun.' His mother helped herself to marmalade. 'Who put you up to it?'

'I thought of it for myself.'

Mrs Bannister raised eyebrows in disbelief and bit her toast. 'I bet it was Laura Thornby. She loves to meddle and she would have told you about the Kennedys' loft.'

Claud did not reply; his head was splitting. He wished he could remember exactly what had been said the night before. He glanced covertly at his parent; she looked, he noticed with unease, like someone who, having dived too steeply, comes up for a welcome gasp of air. 'Did I say anything else?' he queried.

'Just your plans for writing, your market stall, and, oh yes, something about Nicholas Thornby which I didn't catch—'

'Good God, yes! I remember now, he gave me quite a shock—'

'Shock?'

'Well, yes. It's so peculiar. Laura is exactly like her mother and—'

'He is exactly like his sister Emily? They are twins.'

'But Mother, it's creepy, the three of them look like triplets, it—'

'Gave you a turn?'

'God knows why.'

'God is about the only one who does. One should not of course put the blame on *him*. More tea?'

Claud did not feel well enough to ask her to elucidate her ambiguity. He was disgusted to see his hand shake as he passed his cup; she had made a fresh pot as she talked. 'A sure cure,' she had been in the habit of saying to his father, 'for a slight binge.' (Not that Father's binges were ever slight.)

'Mother,' Claud heard himself saying, 'there is no need really for me to move out. I am sorry I said all that - I can perfectly well stay on here, it's—'

'God forbid!' said Margaret Bannister brusquely.

'What?'

'I said, God forbid, darling.' She looked at her son, hardened her heart. 'It is not that I don't love having you, but not permanently. Holidays and visits are nice but,' here she went quite pink, 'you are twenty-three and it is rather marvellous to have my house to myself.'

'And not have people throwing up in the hall.'

'I was not mentioning that.'

'Oh.' So that's why she looked as though coming up for air. She'd found freedom. Freedom from him. Claud felt betrayed. 'Were you pleased when Father lit off?'

'Of course.'

'Gosh.' Claud felt awe.

'I have been thinking of moving for some time. I can get a good price for this house,' Margaret Bannister said cheerfully.

'Moving? What about my laundry?' It was out before he could stop himself.

'There's the launderette. There's what's she called, Maeve?'

'Mavis.'

'Part of the price of independence is dealing with your own dirty linen,' said Margaret Bannister. She got up and began to clear the table. Watching her, Claud wished that for once he could confide in her; he had always been so careful not to, but now— 'I am very sorry about last night,' he began.

'Not to worry, these things happen.'

'I didn't break anything, did I?'

'Not that I know of.' She was dismissive.

'Good – er – um – er . . .'

'What is it, Claud?'

'I just wanted to apologise.' She was feeding the dishwasher plates and cups, just as long ago she had spooned cereal into his infant mouth, patiently mopping when he regurgitated, only the dishwasher was better mannered than he had been. 'I only wanted to apologise,' he repeated.

'I said, not to worry.' She had her back to him.

'We never seem to talk, do we?'

'And whose fault is that?' she snapped. 'You long since made it clear that you resent questions and that your life and friends have nothing to do with me, that your affection is minimal, my uses limited.'

'Oh.'

'Recently it has suited you to live here; possibly you find this place less dull and provincial than you thought. You see it with a fresh eye. I am glad,' she straightened her back and shut the dishwasher, 'that you have the gumption to risk life on your own. You have no roots here, maybe you are growing them? You cannot expect me to hang around while they grow, and water them by doing your laundry. There's a mixed metaphor for a writer. If we never talk, Claud, it is because you have reduced the snub to a fine art.'

Claud pushed his chair back and stood up. 'Thanks for telling me,' he said. 'D'you know once when I was small Dad shouted at me that I would grow up into a completely selfish swine?'

'He must have been drinking.'

'No, I think he was sober.'

'Perhaps he foresaw your future. Writers need to be selfish.'

'I was not at that time proposing to be a writer.'

'Well, whatever.' She fended him off.

'Did he know the Thornbys?'

'We knew them.'

'Are they bad news?'

'– M-m-m'

'I think it was the old man who put a bucket over my head and pushed me down a flight of stairs.'

'That figures.' Margaret Bannister switched on the dishwasher. 'I really hardly know them,' she shouted above the sound of swishing water.

'You must, you have lived here for years.'

'You can live in a place without knowing people.'

Claud sensed that his mother had no intention of enlightening him. 'I only just now noticed Laura,' he said.

'Not surprising, she's scarcely ever here.' His mother's tone increased Claud's interest. 'You are getting to know her now,' she said, glancing at her son obliquely. As she did so he became aware of a similarity; his mother's look matched what he had the day before called sidelong in Laura. Yet he failed to put one and one together to see them as much of an age.

'I would recommend a bath,' said his mother, cutting short his wish to talk. 'A bath that is good and hot, and put a spoonful of Scrubs ammonia in it. It will clear your head wonderfully.'

'You used to say that to Father.'

'One does so repeat oneself.'

He sensed that she was laughing again, that she was a more interesting person than he gave her credit for and that he had missed the chance of knowing her. 'You make me feel lonely,' he shouted above the noise of the dishwasher.

'Writers are solitary people,' she said.

Lying in the bath waiting for his head to clear, Claud reviewed the events of the previous day. Memory was clear up to his arrival at the Old Rectory, after that confused. He remembered reaching the pub where he had asked for a double Scotch to revive his courage. (I really am the most frightful coward, he thought, leaning forward to adjust the hot tap.) Feeling better, he had perhaps unwisely ordered another. (I should have eaten some of that seed cake, he remembered Laura's seed cake.) He heard his voice in the pub saying in confident tones, 'The same again, please,' yet stop, think, wasn't the voice on the verge of being disembodied? Well? It was after that drink that he had glanced towards the door and seen Laura in triplicate. What had caused most alarm and instability was that this was no ordinary triplication – several times at university he had seen double and once in triplicate – what on this occasion terrified was that Laura in triplicate was no run-of-the-mill vision. One emanation, if this was the right word, was male, the other the female who had shut the door of the Old Rectory in his face. Claud's brain, under the influence of his mother's strong tea, aspirin and the fumes of ammonia, clicked into gear. At breakfast just now he had mentioned Nicholas Thornby 'giving him a shock' and now, he recollected, someone in the pub calling out 'Hullo, Nicholas' before the Laura in triplicate wheeled round and left the pub as fast and as silently as it had appeared.

How weird, thought Claud, how peculiar. What were they doing? There were three Lauras: one was her mother, the other this Nicholas. Was it then, he asked himself, that Brian and Susie had come into the bar and that had led to the other and fatal double Scotch? Must have been. Made one think. Claud reached for the soap and began to wash. As he soaped his armpits, he remembered that earlier in Laura's part of the Old Rectory he had called Laura's mother her *doppelgänger*, and Laura at some moment had made reference to what sounded like 'haunts'.

Well, thought Claud, ducking underwater, that explains some of it. He let the water roar agreeably in his ears while he held his breath. I wish my mother had a shower, he thought, sitting up and turning on the cold tap, sponging himself with icy water. Finally he stood up, reached for his bath towel, pulled the plug and dried his torso and legs vigorously while his feet still indulged in the hot water. He then dried his feet one at a time before stepping out onto the bathmat, a slightly old-maidish but commendable habit since it did not leave the mat soggy for the next-comer.

They must, thought Claud, feeling restored and nonchalant, Susie and Brian must have brought me home. Ah well, these things happen, but it still does not explain the bucket over my head, that terrifying bashing and the fall downstairs, does it?

Claud left the bathroom, returned to his bedroom to dress. Yesterday's wear lay scattered. Shoes and one sock by the bed, anorak on the floor, shirt slung over the bedside lamp, jeans. Where the hell are my jeans? Oh dear, at the bottom of the bed, how sordid. And the other sock? Marking a book? Did I try to read? Rather than look further at present Claud turned his back on the bed and found clean clothes neatly arranged in his chest of drawers. What was that his mother had said about the price of independence? Could she mean it? What a viper!

Dressed, Claud shut his bedroom door and trotted downstairs to where he could hear voices in the kitchen. His mother was entertaining Laura.

'Hullo,' said Laura. 'I brought you the things from the attic, as I promised. What a pity you couldn't wait for them. These will help you make a start with your stall; your mother thinks they are lovely.'

'Excellent,' said Margaret Bannister, fingering an assortment of objects and small junk spread on the kitchen table. 'Cracked, of course, some of them, or chipped; could do with a wash or a polish, most of them. Look at this.' She held up a glass. 'Bristol, quite pretty.'

'What did you do to your eye?' asked Laura, ignoring Margaret's denigrating accent. 'What has he done to his eye, Margaret? Your son's got a shiner.'

'I have not asked him,' said Margaret Bannister. 'Look, these nutcrackers work and this spoon might almost be silver, one could clean it.'

'Somebody put a bucket over my head and bashed me,' said Claud. 'Then I fell downstairs.'

Laura raised her eyebrows and looked down her nose. 'You've been listening to Mavis about Northern Ireland,' she said. 'She does go on.'

'Things like that don't happen in this country.' Margaret aligned herself momentarily with Laura. 'I'd say this would have been Bohemian before it was chipped.' She held up a small vase. 'An idea, though, the bucket, for your novel?'

'It's only a little crack, a crack doesn't alter its nationality,' said Laura.

'My head was cracked,' said Claud, persisting. Laura smiled and went on unpacking the contents of a large basket. 'A present from Scarborough,' she said, 'and here's its twin, a present from Lowestoft, a tiny baby's potty. Oh, this shouldn't be here, I'll take it back.'

'What's that?' Margaret was interested.

'Patch box, a good one. Nor should this be here.' She pocketed a silver snuff box. 'But the rest's all yours.' She spread her hands. 'All yours.'

'So is my black eye,' said Claud, 'and I think I have concussion.'

'You'd know if you had concussion,' said Margaret. 'Coffee, Laura? I was going to make a fresh pot. If you had concussion you would see double; it affects your eyesight.'

'I saw in triplicate last night.' Claud stared at Laura. 'Clearly, in threes.'

'I can't drink Nescaff,' said Laura, returning Claud's stare. 'Were you pissed?'

'I never touch the stuff,' said Margaret. 'This is the real thing, want some?'

'Perhaps I won't, I'm late as it is.' Laura reached for her coat. Claud helped her on with it. She was not wearing the Cossack hat today; the back of her neck reminded him of Mavis. 'I'll see you out,' he said.

'Goodbye, Margaret,' said Laura, 'see you when I come again.'

'Where are you going?' Claud followed Laura to her car.

'London.'

'Aren't you helping me with my stall?'

'Haven't I helped you enough?' She got into the car.

'Did you put the bucket over my head?' Claud held onto the car door. 'And bash me?'

'Oh, Claud, don't be an ass.'

'Take me with you.'

'Why should I do that?' Laura switched on the engine.

Claud leaned in through the car window and kissed her cheek. 'Laura—'

'I suggested to your mother that you should give me twenty-five per cent of the sale of that lot.'

'Oh.' He had thought she was giving it gratis.

'It gives you a start, doesn't it? With your part of the profit you can buy more stock to carry on with.' She brushed her hand across her cheek as though his kiss had been a fly.

'Ah—'

'Brian and Susie will show you the ropes.'

'Won't you help me?'

'Shan't be here.'

'But—'

'Mavis doesn't always work mornings, she'll give you a hand.'

'Did you put that bucket over my head? Did I see you in the pub later? With your *doppelgängers*?'

'You may have done.' Laura put the car into gear and drove away.

'Damn you,' Claud yelled after her. 'Bitch.'

'You are getting to be so like your father,' said Margaret when he rejoined her in the kitchen.

'What's that supposed to mean?' Claud was surly.

'He too used to find romantic excuses for alcoholic accidents.'

'I'm not an alcoholic. I'm moving out,' shouted Claud. 'I'm off.'

'He said that too,' said Margaret. 'I hope you are as good as your word.'

Furious with Laura, Claud rounded on his mother. 'You don't believe in me, you have no faith in me, you expect me to be a failure,' he yelled. 'I tell you this, Mother, if I don't make a success of my writing, if I say, because I shall, if I am not recognised, I shall kill myself. Now,' he said bitterly, leaning close to Margaret so that she flinched with pity at the close-up of his black eye, 'now tell me my father also threatened to kill himself—'

'No,' said Margaret, 'no. He died of a heart attack, he—'

'But he did promise to kill himself. I used to hear him. He'd say he'd hang himself, cut his wrists, overdose. I heard him, Mother. He would have, too,' cried Claud, jubilant with rage. 'The heart attack happened first, that's all.'

Margaret turned away. 'We need a vegetable for lunch,' she murmured.

Claud watched her go out into the garden in her thin shoes and start picking brussels sprouts, twisting the tender miniature cabbages off their obscenely thick stalks. She looked thin out there, bending in the cold wind, which made her eyes glitter with tears as her cold fingers fumbled at the vegetables, dropping them into a fold of her apron. She had forgotten to take the colander she usually used.

Claud took the colander from its hook. Should he take it to her?

She came in before he could make up his mind; he put it back on its hook.

'I wonder, did I leave my umbrella here? I was at the concert the other night, Clug's new Quartet, the Roumanian composer, conductor too, so talented and then the Bach—' Martin looked round the hall, rather shabby and sad in daylight. 'A black brolly with malacca handle, a gold band with my grandfather's name on it. Otho Bengough. I put it over there, I think, or maybe not, I was sitting near the back, I—'

'I am only the caretaker, well, cleaner, actually. It's a holiday job before I go on to—' The girl looked pleadingly at Martin with pekinese eyes.

'University,' supplied Martin.

'Polytechnic, actually.' She blushed.

'Just as good,' said Martin. 'Who d'you think would have it? The brolly?'

'It can't have been stolen, though—'

'I wasn't suggesting it had.'

'Of course not, no; Robert, the arts director, would have given it to Emily Thornby to care for until it's claimed. Though why she should be - er.'

'What?'

'Oh, nothing. Oh, well,' the girl blushed deeper, 'it's just that she's such an odd person to put in charge of - er.'

'Lost property?' How very convenient. Was this a sign?

'Yes.'

'Apt to confiscate it for herself?'

'Oh, I didn't say that! No, no, it's just that she's funny, er, well—'

'How is she funny?' Martin probed.

'Well, she's a sort of lost person herself. I mean she doesn't fit any usual category, none of the Thornbys do.' The girl spoke in a rush. 'Actually she's rather terrifying, worse than her brother. Oh, I'll give you their address. Here, if you have a piece of paper I'll write it down. She would never claim to being lost, oh Lord no.'

Martin handed the girl a biro. 'You don't like her.' He found an envelope in his pocket.

'Nobody does.' The girl began writing. 'Except possibly Laura, that's the daughter. I suppose she has to.'

'You have beautiful handwriting.' Martin inspected the envelope.

'Oh,' said the girl, 'thanks. It's no use telephoning them,' she said, 'their phone's out of order, or was. I've written the number just in case, but often they don't bother to answer. You might catch them latish—'

'You seem to know their habits.'

'Their daily lady works for my mother. She seems to like Laura. You may have noticed her at the concert, in a frightfully green dress, I mean green!'

You don't like Laura. 'Thanks a lot,' said Martin,

'I'll try them latish.' He started back towards his car.

'They've got the most amazing dog,' the girl said, following him. 'Nicholas has trained him to "Die for Eastbourne", it's a hoot!'

'Thanks again.' Martin got into his car. The Old Rectory, the girl had written in biro, Uttoxeter Road. Why Uttoxeter? he pondered. This place is miles from there.

'Do be careful of the dog.' The girl stood by the car. 'It bites.'

'Kind of you to warn me.' Martin smiled at the girl.

'Oh,' she said, 'not at all.' She stared at Martin, thinking that he had a kind face, a mouth which curled up at the corners, slaty grey eyes. She wondered whether he was married. 'I am going to study art,' she said. 'I'm too stupid for anything else.'

'I don't think you are stupid. Who put that idea in your head?' Not waiting for an answer, Martin started the engine and drove away. Glancing in the mirror he saw the girl semaphoring that he was heading in the wrong direction. He turned the car at the next intersection and drove back past where she still stood on the steps of the concert hall. As he passed her he waved and shouted, 'Silly me,' but he thought, Silly interfering bitch; he had liked the green dress.

He circled back to the town (the umbrella could wait) to park in a multi-storey car park. From the top deck of the car park there was a magnificent view of the river, the cathedral-sized church, the market square and distant downland. It was a sign of the age, he thought, as he ran down the steps to the street, that car parks like lavatories often had the best views and, like lavatories, he thought, holding his breath, they stank.

Gaining the street, he slackened his pace to saunter

through the town. In the wine shop he dawdled over his choice; in the delicatessen he bought truffle chocolates; in the fruit shop, figs. As he shopped he chatted to the shopkeepers; in the flower shop he chatted while he bought regale lilies. Lastly he spent half an hour browsing in a second-hand bookshop, searching for a book long out of print and engaging the shop owner in desultory converse. Then, laden with carrier bags and the bouquet of lilies, he collected his car and drove fifteen miles to visit his aunt by marriage, Calypso Grant.

'It's not often,' said his aunt, 'that I get a visit from the Bengough branch of Hector's clan. Come in and share my lunch, you are just in time. Shut up!' she said to a large dog which was barking, bowing and wagging its tail. She reached up to kiss Martin's cheek. 'Come in out of the cold.'

'I brought you a bottle or two, some chocs and some figs.' Martin returned her kiss. 'And these.' He presented the lilies.

'How extravagant,' said Calypso. 'I love extravagance. What can I give in return? We will eat the figs with one of Willy Guthrie's smoked hams. You know he married a girl called Poppy Carew?'

'I was at the wedding.' Martin followed his aunt into the house.

'So you were. We'll eat in the kitchen.'

'I need a little info, Aunt. I've lost my umbrella, mislaid would put it better, and the people who have it are—'

'Are what? Are who?'

'Some people called Thornby.'

Calypso laughed. 'Everybody knows the Thornbys. They are poison, surely your snooping told you that?'

'You know my little ways.' Martin watched Calypso

lay a place for him. 'They seem to have a daughter who wears green.'

'But in my opinion, for what it's worth, she is not poisonous,' said Calypso.

Martin asked: 'Shall I open a bottle? She was at a concert I went to.'

Calypso handed him a corkscrew and began carving ham which stood on a dish on the kitchen table. 'I bet you are hungry,' she said. 'The daughter is called Laura, no doubt you found that out. She has a business in London, no doubt you found that out too—' There was a lack of approval in her tone which Martin chose to ignore.

'Would you know her address?' he asked. 'In London?'

'No, but I have the telephone number somewhere.'

'That will do. Thanks, Aunt.' Martin sat down to his ham.

'I hope you are not in a rush to leave,' said Calypso. 'Share out the figs, love.'

'I have some time off.' Martin chose the best figs for his aunt.

'Stay the night,' she suggested. 'There's a bed made up.'

'May I? There's something I have to do later this evening.'

'Nefarious?' asked Calypso.

'Just some ends to tie—'

'I like Laura Thornby,' said Calypso coldly.

'I have no intention of hurting her,' said Martin huffily.

'That's all right, then. I'll give you a key in case I've gone to bed when you get back.'

'What made you think I might hurt her?' In spite of himself Martin was edgy.

Calypso chewed her ham, sipped her wine. 'Have you really mislaid Otho's umbrella? I remember it well. Never, of course, playing the part of a Trojan horse.' She glanced at Martin, who was peeling a fig. 'Your grandfather never carried it furled. It looked pretty funny flopping loose when otherwise he was so exactly turned out; he had such a courteous way of offering its shelter when it rained at the races.'

'He loved pretty girls.' Martin ignored the suggestion of the Trojan horse. Calypso always made one's most delicate endeavours look clumsy.

Calypso smiled, accepting the refusal. 'I don't know what he would have been like as a lover, but he was excellent company.'

Martin, remembering his old aunt's racy reputation, ventured: 'He sympathised with me once for being too young for you and said that he alas was too old; I was about six at the time. It made an impression. Why don't you bridle, Aunt?' he teased.

'Bridling is not my line. More ham?'

'Please.' Martin passed his plate.

'I hope you will soon give up your unsporting occupation and find a girl of the right age,' said Calypso, referring obliquely to Martin's profession.

'I thought unsought advice was against your principles,' answered Martin. Secretly he agreed with E. M. Forster that it was more important to be loyal to one's friends than one's country.

Calypso laughed. 'A slip, my dear. The great improvement in your cousin Willy since he married Poppy makes me hopeful for others.'

'I shall bear your concern in mind,' said Martin. 'I am due in Washington next week.'

'Another job?' Martin sensed an unsniffed sniff.

'Won't your bachelorhood be at serious risk? Those American girls are delicious.'

'It has survived on previous assignments.' Martin met his aunt's eye.

'All right.' She tacitly admitted that she had teased him enough. 'All right.'

Later that evening, driving through a downpour of rain along the road to the Old Rectory, Martin thought it was pleasant to be free of Clug. What really bugs me, he thought, hesitating in the rain in the darkness of the Old Rectory drive, is why a woman like Laura Thornby should have bothered with Clug when there was so obviously no future in it?

Standing in the shelter of the laurel hedge he reviewed such facts as he had gleaned that day. Brought up by her mother and uncle, school fees paid by someone called Ned Peel, who might or might not be her father. A wickedly mischievous child who had turned into a woman no one seemed to know much about; there was the impression that she was more feared than liked, that she was remarkably secretive. I know why I am secretive, Martin thought, why should she be? There was the emphasis on her wearing bright colours, a linking of her name with Ned Peel's son Christopher (old, very old history this). Her parent was considered a handicap, well, that's not unusual. 'A bit lonely, or perhaps I should say solitary.' The man in the bookshop. 'Not someone you'd care to tangle with.' The woman in the flower shop.

Encouraged by a fresh burst of rain Martin shook off his hesitation and rang the Old Rectory bell. There was an instant barking uproar from a well-lit hall. Martin waited, then rang again. The barking increased but nobody came. He lifted the letterbox flap and squinted in. Across a hallway he could see an umbrella stand and in it his forebear's umbrella. Some attempt had been made to furl it and it looked extraordinarily disreputable. His view was blotted out by snapping teeth and hot doggy breath accompanied by choking barks.

Martin withdrew and began circling the house; many people he knew sat asking to be burgled as they watched loud television. At the back of the house light streamed out from a ground floor window; there was a door with a knocker. He knocked. Since nobody came he pushed and the door swung open to show a large room which smelled of woodsmoke, flowers, garlic, pepper. Martin called, 'Hullo? Anybody there?'

A small cat stood up, stretched, lay down again by the fire. At the front of the house the dog still gave an occasional token bark.

If I walk through to the front and retrieve my brolly, I could call it a day, Martin thought. Then he heard a car's tyres crunching on the gravel at the front, the dog's bark changing to a joyful note and voices raised, one of them in song.

'Roll me over, in the clover, roll me over and do it again.' Quavering, old, drunk. 'Help me out of this, help me out, help!'

'Wait,' said a woman's voice.

'I want to go back to the pubby pub pub.' Another voice, female, also old.

Martin came softly round the house. A car with its doors open, two old people struggling tipsily, a woman opening the front door, the dog rushing out to slaver over the old people. The woman saying, 'Come on, you terrible disgraces, that's the last time I take you on a pub crawl.' She tried to lever the old man out of the car. His legs splayed out, folded, he collapsed onto the ground. 'Oh, God,' said the woman. The old woman was trying to get into the driving seat from the back of the car. 'No you don't,' said the woman Martin recognised as Laura and snatched away the car keys. The old woman lashed out with her fist and toppled out of the car. Now both old people were on the ground. The dog lavished licks on their faces. 'Oh, Bonzo, Bonzo, Bonzo,' they chorused, 'you love us, boozy Bonzo boy.'

'Can I help?' Martin stepped forward.

'Thanks,' said Laura, startled.

'No, no, no, no, no,' shouted the old man. 'Gross interference of personal liberty.'

'Put him on the sofa in the drawing-room.' Laura raised her voice above the old man's.

Martin caught the old man up and manoeuvred him into the house, deposited him as told, and went back to assist Laura.

'Stop it, Ma, stop it.' Laura tried to avoid wildly flailing arms.

'No child of mine,' shouted the old woman. 'Freak! An asp, an asp, an asp.'

'You never cherished me much.' Laura was patient. 'Come on, Ma, don't be impossible, you'll get soaked.'

'My name is Emily Thornby,' shouted the old woman. 'Don't call me Ma.' She aimed a blow at Laura's face. Martin caught her wrists. 'Where shall we put her?'

'On the other sofa.' Laura switched on a light. What a civilised venue, thought Martin, looking about him.

Emily bit his thumb. 'Ouch!' Martin snatched his hand away.

'Drawn blood?' asked the old man, sitting up and looking interested. 'You want to be careful of drunks.'

He lay back, clutching Bonzo to his bosom. Bonzo snuffled and licked his neck. (What a disgusting animal, thought Martin.) 'You love us, Bonzo, even if she doesn't; she has fallen in love with a spotted youth, Bonzo, brought shame on my grey hairs.'

'They've mostly fallen out,' shouted Emily from her sofa. 'Fancy blacking that poor boy's eye; mind this one, Nicholas, he looks dangerous. Who are you?' She stared belligerently at Martin.

Keeping out of reach, wrapping his thumb in his handkerchief, Martin said: 'I am extremely sorry. I was passing this way and thought I would collect my umbrella, which I left at the concert.' (Why am I apologising?)

'Umbrella,' said Emily, 'umbrella?'

Nicholas groaned. 'God, I haven't been so pissed for years. Thank you, darling.' Laura was taking off his shoes.

'Just put some logs on the fire,' she said to Martin, 'he'll go to sleep in a minute and so will she.' She moved across to Emily and removed her shoes.

'Lovely.' Emily wiggled her toes.

'Rugs,' muttered Laura and went away to return with rugs which she swathed round the old people, propping their heads on cushions. Her actions were tender and considerate. 'You are not all that wet,' she said, 'I'd never get you up to bed.'

Martin watched her. She rearranged the logs he had put on the fire and watched it blaze, then stood looking down at the old people swaddled now in rugs, lying quietly. 'Better leave the light on in case they get dizzy,' she murmured.

Nicholas gave a loud snore and let his arms fall away from the dog, who now leapt from his master's arms and approached Martin, snarling.

Terrified but inspired Martin shouted, 'Die for Eastbourne!'

Bonzo rolled over and lay flat.

Laura let out a whoop of laughter: 'Oh, how? Oh, where did you? Oh, ho, ho, ho ho.' She pressed her hand against her side. 'Oh, ho, ho, ho, ho, it hurts.'

'I will just get my umbrella,' said Martin, 'then I'd better push off.' He felt acutely embarrassed. This was not how he had visualised introducing himself.

'Yes,' said Laura, 'yes.' Her eyes brimming, she followed Martin into the hall. 'Of course,' she said weakly. She was still giggling uncontrollably. 'Your umbrella.'

Martin took the umbrella from the stand and said, 'Goodbye.'

'Goodbye,' said Laura, pulling herself together as she opened the door for him to step out into the rain.

Martin opened the umbrella and held it up; as the rain pattered down onto it, he was surprised to find he was trembling.

His aunt was still up when he got back. 'Did you find what you were looking for?' she asked, switching off the television.

'I don't know,' said Martin. 'I got bitten.'

'You'll find Elastoplast in the kitchen,' said Calypso. 'Goodnight, my dear, I am going to bed. What a risky occupation yours is.'

The tone of his aunt's voice, thought Martin, dabbing antiseptic on his wound, exactly matched the smile Laura had given him as he left. In America women did not ridicule with such diabolical accuracy, they were kind to the weaker sex.

'I suppose you talked to Ann Kennedy?' Calypso called from the top of the stairs.

'Who is Ann Kennedy?' Martin answered unguardedly.

'Not a very thorough snoop, are you?' his Aunt Calypso mocked. He heard her go into her bathroom and turn on the taps; above the sound of rushing water he heard her voice. 'She rents her loft.' There was no time, thought Martin dismally as he wound Elastoplast round his thumb, to investigate Calypso's hint. He must leave for the States.

'Pull, for crissakes,' Claud yelled, 'pull.'

'I think - I am - doing - my guts - an injury.'

Mavis heaved at the belt of webbing strung under the calor gas heater. 'We must get it up before Mum comes in,' she gasped. 'She's terrified of fire.'

On the ladder Claud got his shoulder under the stove and gave it a final heave through the trap-door. The stove toppled over, knocking Mavis onto her back. Claud came up through the trap, righted the stove and trundled it into place on its castors. His legs trembled from the strain of lifting. 'Now the place looks civilised,' he said, looking at his arrangement of books, typewriter, the box of manuscript, biros, pencils, india rubber, ruler, dictionary, paper clips. 'Ready for the off,' he said. 'If I type out my two paragraphs and sixteen sentences again, I can carry on from there. Brilliant.' He stood looking at his new domain and wound the belt of webbing round his fist. 'Where does this come from?' He looked down at Mavis flopped on the floor.

'I borrowed it from the undertaker.'

'Oh.' Claud laid the webbing down quickly. How many coffins had this webbing abandoned to the worms? 'Oh—'

'I'm exhausted.' Mavis rolled off her back, crawled to the mattress and sank onto it. 'Oof,' she said, 'this is comfortable.' She still wore her overcoat. She lay and watched Claud light the stove. 'If you shut the trap-door,' she said, 'we can see how long it takes to warm the loft.'

'Did Laura have one of these up here?' Claud shut the trap-door.

'She had an electric fire. She ran a flex down into the room below; Mum wasn't pleased when she found out.'

'Does she come up here?' Claud shrank from the thought of invasion by Mrs Kennedy.

'No, but she noticed when her electricity bill shot up.'

'Well, that won't happen with this.' Claud patted the gas stove. 'Did Laura have to repay your mother?'

'I can't remember. Hey, it would have been much easier to get that stove up without the cylinder.' Mavis chirruped with laughter

'Now she tells me.' Claud stood looking down at Mavis on her back on the bed, Laura's bed, the one she had left here. He rather envied Laura's theft of electricity, tried to imagine Laura on the bed, but it was Mavis there showing her bright teeth, eyes half closed, muffled in that bloody coat. She had dark lashes and eyebrows, he noticed; if they had been pale like many redheads, it would have put paid to her looks. He sat beside her on the bed. 'Why do you keep your coat on?'

Mavis held the lapels close together. 'I like it.'

'Wrap me in it, too.' He stretched out beside her. 'You smell nice.' He nuzzled her neck. 'You don't wear scent, do you?'

'No,' said Mavis, 'no, it's all me.'

Claud kissed her mouth. 'You taste nice too.'

'Tell me the story of your novel.'

'I've got an erection.'

Mavis clutched her coat about her and crossed her legs.

'Oh, for the happy days of carefree love!' Claud accepted her refusal

'That generation don't look any happier than us, I can't see that it makes all that difference really.'

'It's the idea—'

'Shouldn't you direct your energies into intellectual activity? Sublimate.'

'What have you been reading?' Claud inserted his hand between the buttons of the coat and started peregrinating towards Mavis' breasts. 'Where are they?'

'Higher up.'

'What a lot of clothes you wear.'

'I feel the cold.'

'The stove is warming us nicely, let me in.'

'No.'

'All right.' He lay beside her. The effort of moving his belongings to the attic had been strenuous. He began to feel sleepy in the increasing warmth. 'The shock of being thrown out of the parental home was traumatic,' he murmured.

'That's not the story your mother told my mum. She helped you pack, ironed your shirts for the last time, bought you new bath towels.'

'What a literal girl you are.'

'It will be useful for your novel, though; are all suggestions gratefully received?'

'Not really. I have to work it out for myself; the new schema is one no one has ever tried before.'

'Is that so.' Mavis in her overcoat sounded sceptical. 'What's so original about it?'

'It's about my mother.'

'And?'

'Her love life.'

'Her love life?'

'You are not to tell anyone.' The scent of Mavis' flesh filled Claud with dangerous indiscretion; her exertions had made her perspire, which curiously enhanced her attraction. Again he set his hand to explore the labyrinth of garments, fumbling up towards her breasts from the waistband of her jeans. 'However many layers of clothes have you got on?' he asked in irritation as he unbuttoned her coat.

'Vest, tee-shirt, shirt and sweater. Your hand is somewhere between the vest and the tee-shirt.'

'You sound like the guide to Hampton Court maze.'

'Go on about your mother.'

Claud withdrew his hand. 'She's past the age for ordinary sex, right?'

'Is that so?'

'For the purpose of my novel it is.'

'Okay, go on.' Mavis resettled her clothes, rebuttoning the coat so that should he be so minded Claud would have to start again from scratch.

Claud folded his arms behind his head. 'She is in love with her machines.'

'Her what?' Mavis reared up on an elbow.

'Her dishwasher, washing machine, spin dryer, mixer. They are all more real to her than a man's penis, she has a special relationship with her microwave.'

'Your mother hasn't got a microwave.'

'Oh, Mavis!' Claud rolled suddenly on top of her, staring at her eye to eye. He could kiss her mouth and throat, but added now to her many layers of clothing were his own shirt and jersey. 'I don't believe anyone has been confronted by so much preventive clothing for years and years.'

'I am inaugurating a new age of mysterious femininity,' said Mavis, her mouth against his mouth. 'You are terribly heavy and I am now too hot.'

'Take some of it off then.'

'No fear.'

'New form of contraception, eh?'

'Yup.'

'I get it, avoidance of our helpful friend?'

'Might be—'

Claud rolled off her. Tenderly he buttoned the overcoat up to her chin. 'I shall start work first thing after breakfast tomorrow.' (Susie had said Mavis' eyes were like jade.)

'Is Mum providing?'

'No, I shall eat at a caff or the wine bar when I can afford it so that you can serve me.'

'Not tomorrow. Tomorrow is market day. Your stall, remember?'

'Oh shit,' said Claud, 'shit.'

Mavis pulled up the trap-door and stepped down onto the ladder. 'I wonder what Laura really got up to in this loft,' she said.

As Mavis disappeared Claud felt the space she had occupied flooded by Laura. Why on earth, what had possessed him to tell Mavis about his mother's machine lovers? Surely only Laura's ear, if any, was the one to confide in? Furiously he kicked out at Mavis' head as it disappeared, missed.

At some point during his first night in the Kennedys' loft, tossing restlessly on a bed new to him, Claud realised with chagrin that his hero with the second-hand Alfa Romeo would not fit the scenario of his mother's mechanical loves. In real life Margaret Bannister used a car to reach A from B. She did not consider a car as anything other than a rather boring means of locomotion. It was with household machines that she had rapport. There was the mixer which would only work for her (I know its little quirks), the Hoover which regurgitated particular forms of dust and refused to ingest spiders, the spin drier which inspired her to raise her voice in song, the washing machine and dishwasher which were as children to be fed, each its own diet. She had, too, a pretty funny relationship with her electric whisk. Would it be possible to weave the whisk into the novel with some esoteric sexual connotation? Sexuality and his mother hardly gelled in Claud's mind but Come on, he urged himself, I am a writer, aren't I? I should be able to tease that idea into shape. I am not writing about my living parent, she is merely the blueprint, the *toile* for the garb of my story. (I must remember not to use phrases like garb for story, they are sickeningly pretentious.)

Unable to sleep, Claud got out of bed and padded barefoot to the table. The pile of paper reproached mutely. With the obstinacy of a procrastinating child it stood between him and progress. He snatched up the heap of paper and tore it across. What he had written would never see print. Just think, he told himself shivering part with cold, part with emotion, what Laura would say were she to set eyes on it. Not for Laura heroes with Alfa Romeos or heroines with, yes he had written it, long legs, wide apart violet eyes, high breasts and tight little bottoms. It's enough to make any intelligent person puke, let alone Laura. What could I have been thinking of?

Claud prised open the window and scattered the shredded bits of paper into the night. Laura need never know. She would appreciate the woman based on his mother and her mechanical familiars, she might even respect his work. I shall dedicate the novel to Laura, Claud promised himself as he closed the window. He went back to lie on the bed, the bed she had installed in this loft when seeking privacy and escape in adolescence.

Half-regretting his violent act Claud thought, What an awful waste of paper. Then, My God, it's market day, I must leap up and set up my stall so that I can earn the money to pay for more paper. I owe it to Laura, my muse. Now, now, he muttered, crawling reluctantly out of bed (I was just beginning to get warm again), don't start calling Laura your muse, that's a sure way to get kicked in the teeth. Taking care not to make a noise, Claud opened the trapdoor and, creeping down the ladder, tiptoed to the bathroom.

He was halfway through shaving when the bathroom door snapped open and Mavis, tightly wrapped in her overcoat, came in. 'What on earth are you doing?'

'Shaving. It's my first day with my stall.'

'What on earth for? None of the stall-holders shave in the morning.'

'I am shaving. I am different.'

'What on earth do you want to be different for?'

'Just get out of here, Mavis, and leave me alone.'

'What on earth for?'

'Mavis, if you say that just once more, I'll cut your throat.'

'What on—'

'I will, Mavis.'

Mavis laughed. 'The kettle's boiled, I've made tea, or d'you prefer coffee?'

'Tea. What on earth are you doing up at this hour? Shit, it's catching.'

'I am going to help you as it's your first day. I know the market people.'

'Oh—'

'I can introduce you, show you the way things get done.'

Claud grunted.

'You don't sound very pleased or grateful. I have kept a stall myself from time to time.'

'What on—'

'To make a bob or two, dummy.'

'Aah.' Claud rinsed his razor. 'I have my stock ready,' he said. 'I've priced it, stuck labels on the bits and pieces.'

'Clever! Pete will come and look it over.'

'Who's Pete?'

'Keeps an antique stall. You'd better be careful not to undercut him, he can be touchy. So can Gladys.'

'Does she have an antique stall too?'

'Yes.'

'Then what on earth am I doing with one?'

Mavis suppressed a grin at the repetition. 'The more antique stalls the better, stupid. People come every week to look for junk. If it's any good, it finds its way to London. The dealers come. You'll get to know them.'

'Ah.'

'You will put them in your books. Perhaps you've thought of that?'

Laura had; Laura had pointed out his stall would be useful copy. Claud asked, 'Any stalls selling machinery?'

'Such as what?'
'Household machines.'
'There's one that sells old fridges and mixers, ancient mangles, that sort of thing. Collectors' pieces. Why?'
'Just interested.'
'When we've set up your stall, you can look round, get to know where everybody is. I'll mind your stall, if you don't take too long, until I go to work.'
'Thanks.' Claud followed Mavis to the kitchen where she gave him tea. As he drank he eyed Mavis, wondering whether there might be a place for her in his novel, but always as he watched her it was Laura who was superimposed, the dark woman blotting her out, the two obliterating the memory of another girl, a girl he did not wish to think about from his recent past.

Claud enjoyed the early bustle of the market, the setting up of stalls, the unloading of vans, the disjointed conversations between people who knew each other well yet had not met for a week. Everybody seemed to know Mavis. 'Hi, Mavis, how's the theatre then?' 'Got a star part yet?' 'Still on the dole?' 'Resting?' 'Never! Working in the old wine bar? See you later then, after market.'
Mavis showed him how to set up the trestles, found him a place next to Brian and Susie 'Pure uncontaminated organically grown fruit and veg'. He was glad of their proximity, amused that Mavis, testing the air with a wet finger, chose a place upwind. She had brought a paisley shawl ('Don't sell this, it belongs to Mum') which she spread over the trestle table, then helped him arrange his wares. As predicted

Pete came across to view, followed by Gladys. Neither Pete, who was bearded and bespectacled, nor Gladys, who had tight white curls and awful lipstick, did more than nod when Mavis introduced Claud. They stared at Claud's things making rapid, but minute, inventory. Pete picked up a china mug with a floral design: 'I have one like this. I've marked it seventeen pounds.'

'What have I put on mine?'

'Sixteen.'

'I'll mark it up then.' (I am cautious, not cowardly.)

'Good boy,' said Gladys. The lipstick had spread onto her teeth.

Pete laughed, his face transformed. 'Mine's a bit chipped,' he said. 'Some wally may buy both.' He wandered back to his own stall, taking Gladys with him.

By eight thirty the market was filling up with serious shoppers, housewives anxious to buy the cream of the fruit and vegetables, choose the freshest fish and best cuts of meat; they heaped their baskets and scurried back to their cars, making room for another class of shopper who came to saunter round the stalls, pick over the second-hand clothes, wander among the aisles of stalls picking things up, putting them down again with no proper intention of buying. Rather they came to meet their friends, exchange news and gossip. Small children ran about getting lost, getting found, tripping over the market dogs, who milled around undecided whether to fight or romp, searching always with sniffing noses for a possible bitch on heat. A lame girl pushed a trolley selling mugs of coffee and slices of dubious pizza; there were several buskers, none properly out of earshot of the other, and a man with matted hair selling roast chestnuts. Claud began to enjoy himself.

Mavis disappeared to work in the wine bar; Brian and Susie were busy at their stall. Today Susie wore mittens. Her little pink fingers snipped and snapped up the vegetables, weighing them on the scales, wrapping them in the recycled paper bags. She dazzled her customers with her smile, flashing her neat little teeth. Claud noticed that as she weighed the carrots or potatoes she smiled into the eyes of her customer while a straying finger depressed the scale just a little, just enough, he calculated with respect, to make a considerable increase in her profit. He wondered whether large and burly Brian was party to this trick.

Customers lingered by his stall, putting on their spectacles, peering at the price tags, picking things up, putting them down, moving away, coming back to look a second time. A woman offered Claud sixteen pounds for the mug he had marked up to seventeen; they made a deal at sixteen fifty. Claud felt elated; this was his first sale. He felt he had arrived. He wrapped the mug tenderly in newspaper, took the money.

Contrapuntally while minding his stall he let his mind dwell on his novel. He saw his mother lingering at the stall which sold old household tools. She turned the handle of a frightful old mangle, chatted to the stall-holder. Was she tempted? What part could an Edwardian mangle play in her life? Claud watched his mother and exulted. Laura will love my book; she must be the first to read it. He daydreamed by his stall in the busy market of a crisp and finished manuscript.

'What are you asking for this?' It was one of Laura's doubles; he held a spoon, his thumb over the price tag.

'The price is written on it.'

'This spoon has my family's crest on it. I wonder

how it got here?' Almost he accused, peering with Laura's dark eyes.

Claud took the spoon from him, looked at the tag: 'Six pounds fifty. Sterling silver.'

'Plate, actually, it's plate.' Laura's double denigrated the spoon, replaced it on the stall. Claud felt the hairs of his neck rise or, he told himself, they rose metaphorically.

'Hullo, Nicholas.' Claud's mother had come up behind him. 'How are you and Emily? How is Laura?'

'We are all so-so, just about so-so.'

Claud was as glad as he had sometimes been as a child to see his mother. 'Hullo, Mother. Can I sell you something?' He felt an unusual need to keep her close to him.

'I have been looking at that old kitchen machinery. D'you think it still works? Fascinating stuff.'

'Is this your son, Margaret? D'you think he's been pinching our spoons? He's got one here with our crest on it. I'm sure it's ours.'

'I hardly think so, Nicholas. I'd no idea you had a crest. Whatever next, should I bow and curtsey? Why don't you buy it?'

Nicholas Thornby moved away. 'That's a mischievous old man,' said Margaret.

'M-m-m.'

'Laura's uncle, or so they say.'

'What else could he be?' asked Claud. 'The likeness is striking.'

'What indeed,' said Margaret Bannister.

'Do you think the spoon was his? Most of this stuff comes from Laura; she brought it from their attic.' Claud felt uneasy.

'Then don't let on. Let him buy it if he wants it back.' Claud was heartened by his mother's robust attitude.

'I think he may have been responsible for my black eye,' Claud whispered.

'Oh, I wouldn't go as far as that,' Margaret demurred. She wanted to ask him whether he was enjoying his new venture, but did not want to seem interfering. She was afraid of embarrassing her son; he was such a touchy fellow. She felt she should buy something from his stall, but all the little objects repelled her. She felt, standing by his stall, that she was barging in on his independence. She would do better to move away. 'I am planning to sell all my outmoded kitchen gadgets to that man over there,' she said.

Claud gaped. In his novel she cherished her gadgets, her life was ruled by them; she did not get rid of them. He felt a sharp pang of abandonment.

Margaret went on, 'I have so much junk; I shall unload it on him and there's plenty about the house that you may like for your stall.'

'That will be lovely,' said Claud dully.

It won't be lovely, it will be a nuisance, thought Margaret. She had no confidence in herself as a parent. Other people seem to be at ease with their children, she thought, why can't I? 'I shall have a grand clearance, a clean sweep when I move,' she said, pretending to be bold.

Claud gasped. He had not realised that her departure was imminent; he had visualised it months, maybe years, ahead, that meanwhile she would be around to provide ideas for the novel. Damn her, he thought, can't she see I need her? Then why can't I tell her? If she were Laura, it would be simple. He watched his mother as she moved away.

'I'll have that spoon.' Nicholas Thornby was back. 'But I shan't give you more than a fiver. It must have been stolen from us, by one of our dailies perhaps.'

'Six pounds fifty,' said Claud. 'Perhaps it was not a daily.' He looked Nicholas in the eye.

'Oh, all right.' Nicholas produced the money from his wallet. 'Twice robbed,' he said. 'Don't wrap it up.'

Claud took the money and handed over the spoon. He was amused to see that Nicholas had chosen the most worn note from his wallet. 'You gave me this black eye,' he said, indicating the bruise, which over a period of a week had faded from purple to greenish yellow.

'I wish I had,' said Nicholas Thornby, 'by which I mean that I would wish I had if you had stolen my spoon, if you can follow a convoluted train of thought.'

'I think I can just about manage,' said Claud. He put the dirty note in his hip pocket.

He sold no more that morning and presently packed up his stall and joined Brian, Susie and other traders for lunch in the wine bar. They all sat round a table while Mavis took their orders, standing graceful and pliant beside the table, reminding Claud of the first morning when he had sat there with Laura. Thinking of Laura he hardly noticed Mavis' appetising body in its nylon overall appearing for once without the overcoat. If he had bothered to look he would have seen Mavis' nipples pointing perkily under the nylon as she breathed, but his mind's eye only saw Laura who was not there. He wished he was sitting alone with Laura so that he could tell her that he was regaining some of the confidence lost with the failed exam and the difficulties with Amy. He had not mentioned the failed exam, it no longer mattered; it was the moral disintegration of his failure with Amy which had significance. Thinking of Laura he endowed her with more power than she had, supposing that she had understood his trouble when she urged him to leave home, to write, to keep a stall, that she wasn't taking an interest for amusement's sake but really cared about him, knew about the confidence Amy had snatched from him so ruthlessly, so cruelly. 'Damn and blast Amy,' he spoke out loud.

'Who is Amy?' asked Brian, looking up from his pizza. 'Anyone we know?'

Claud did not answer but ordered an Irish coffee, catching Mavis by the skirt as she passed their table, calling her Maeve. 'Mavis, my name is Mavis.' She smacked his hand and went away to place his order.

'I am sorry,' Claud called after her, 'I failed to recognise you without your coat.'

Watching Claud settle into a routine at the market precipitated Margaret's plan to sell up and move. She did not trust him to stay in the Kennedys' loft; it was too basic. The bohemian glamour might soon wear off. She could see him moving back into her house bringing habits which did not fit with hers, moods which could be trying.

Since her husband's departure she had secretly looked forward to the time when, his education complete, Claud would flit into the outer world, leaving her to do whatever she wished with an uncluttered conscience. Now she felt threatened. Claud looked like settling in the town he had affected to despise all the years they had lived in it. He was making friends with locals who up to now had not been worth his trouble. Being herself naturally unsociable Margaret had, when her husband embarrassed her with his quarrelsome drinking, kept aloof from people. When he left her she remained withdrawn; his absence made no difference. As he grew up Claud had clearly found home boring, had preferred to spend holidays away with friends, sulked when he had to be at home. She knew that he thought her dull; indeed, in adolescence, he often said so. She had never anticipated his wanting to live near or with her when he left university.

She now saw her solitude at risk. She blamed herself for introducing him to Laura at the concert, so brilliant against the drab background. She felt threatened when, several times during his first week in the loft, Claud dropped in to share her meals, bringing with him his laundry to feed her washing machine, taking the opportunity to have a bath. Her hot water system was, it seemed, more reliable than the Kennedys'. He brought his new friends, Brian and Susie, for drinks; asked whether he could bring Mavis for supper, making it impossible for her to refuse. A mild hint she dropped about independence and doing his own washing he ignored. He was, he said, working hard on his novel, getting inspiration from local colour; he looked round the kitchen when he said this, fingering her electric whisk or fidgeting with the mixer in a way which made her uneasy.

Irrationally Margaret blamed Laura for all this. Mavis, a more obvious cause of potential trouble, worried her not at all; it was the idea of Laura that caused angst. However private and withdrawn she had been during the years she had lived in the neighbourhood, she had not escaped hearing that the Thornbys had a reputation. The old brother and sister were said to be odd, and Laura a mischief-monger; nobody knew why she had not married or what she did when she was elsewhere. She had rented the Kennedys' loft for many years, but latterly had taken over the back premises of the Old Rectory, building a brick partition between herself and the old people. Some person had joked that she had created not a granny flat but a manic's flat. Margaret was on Christian name terms with the Thornbys, as everybody was with everyone these days, a habit caught from America; she greeted them cheerily in public but had no wish to enlarge her acquaintance.

So Margaret made a date with the house agent; her house was eminently saleable. She invited the man who kept the machine and tool stall in the market to call. He came next day and went away with most of her kitchen equipment. The cheque he gave her surprised her by its substance.

She sorted her clothes, ruthlessly reducing her wardrobe to essentials. Oxfam benefited, and the jumble sales more so.

She invited the second-hand booksellers to browse among her surplus books. Systematically she ransacked the house for objects suitable for Claud's stall, packing them in cardboard boxes which she stowed in the boot of her car.

As she stripped the house of belongings, she cleaned it, erasing the patina it had acquired from her occupation, stripping it of its character, preparing it for the imprint of new owners.

When the estate agent brought some people to view, she was in the garden getting it tidy for a spring she would not be there to see. She answered the would-be buyers' questions politely, but when they asked her how she could bear to leave such a charming neighbourhood, such an adorable convenient little house, she did not think it was any of their business and further questions froze.

She knew she was running away and felt guilty. Guilt cemented her determination to escape Claud.

When the house agent telephoned the same evening to tell her the people were prepared to buy at the asking price on condition they could move in immediately, she accepted the offer with relief. The prospect of moving away was rejuvenating. She looked forward to it with joy.

'Goodness, what are you up to?' Laura, returned from London, stood in the porch. She looked over Margaret's shoulder into the hall, interested and inquisitive. 'Someone told me you were moving,' she said. 'I wondered whether your house would suit some friends of mine who are househunting. And another thing, have you any furniture you are parting with that I might—' she let the sentence drop.

'Why don't you come in?' Margaret stood aside. She guessed that the househunting friends were imaginary, but it was possible Laura was interested in furniture; in any case she could not stop Laura's inquisitiveness without being rude. 'Come in,' she repeated.

'Thanks,' said Laura. 'It's a super house, how can you bear to leave it?'

'Quite easily.' Let Laura discover for herself that the house was sold.

'Where shall you live?'

Margaret ignored this. 'There's a chest of drawers in Claud's room I shall sell. I definitely won't keep that.'

'May I look at it? Where did you say you will live?'

'I didn't. D'you mind looking round on your own? I'm rather busy packing things for Claud's stall.'

'Of course not. Sorry to interrupt. Has he sold the stuff I gave him?'

'Why don't you ask him?'

'I shall. Okay if I look round?'

'Please do.' Margaret moved towards the stairs. Let her pry on her own. Why should Claud be beholden to this woman? She watched her climb the stairs, then took a tray and stacked it with a tea set she had thought that morning she would keep. Now she decided to give it to Claud. As she wrapped the cups and saucers in newspaper she heard Laura moving about and thought, not for the first time, that while the outer walls of the cottage were thick, the inside was by no means soundproof. In the past she had heard much she would rather not, not only from her husband but from Claud, too. She could leave these echoes behind.

'How much do you want for the chest?' Laura rejoined her.

Margaret named her price.

'Okay, fine, I'll have it. I need one. I found this when I pulled out the drawers.' Laura handed an envelope to Margaret. 'Snaps of a girl. She's pretty. Friend of Claud's?'

Margaret took the envelope, looked at the snaps. She knew at once that this was an oblique sign from Claud. She did not recognise the girl. This would be the girl he had so often telephoned, who had wrung him out like a dishcloth, taken to hanging up on him, ceased to exist in his life.

'Oh, that's Amy,' she said, furious to feel her neck flush, her voice alter. 'Well, like a cup of tea? I was about to make one.'

'Why not? Thanks.' Laura followed Margaret to the kitchen. 'You'd never seen that girl, had you?' Laura sat at the kitchen table. 'I suppose he was in love with her. I suppose she chucked him. Badly hurt, was he?'

She had made him fail his exams. This was some sort of message; obviously he couldn't bear to talk about the girl, the girl he had called Amy, shouting the name into the unresponsive telephone. Laura was still speaking. 'But you never met her, did you?'

'How do you know?' It popped out.

'Your expression. An oh dear that's cat's-mess face.'

Margaret laughed. 'It always gives me away. You haven't got friends looking for a house, have you? You are interested in Claud.'

'That makes two with intuition. Yes, I find him interesting, easily hurt I'd say, vulnerable. One wouldn't want to hurt him.'

'I wouldn't suggest you would. How old are you?'

'Forty-five.'

'I am fifty-five. I had him when I was thirty-two, rather old to start a family.'

'Which makes him twenty-three.'

'Yes, poor boy.'

'Poor boy, poor boy,' Laura laughed. 'He needs boosting, jollying up, that's all.'

'I've tried. Failed lamentably.'

'Your heart isn't in it.'

'My heart is battle fatigued,' said Margaret.

Laura grinned; she enjoyed teasing people. She watched Margaret making tea, putting out mugs, bending to take milk from the refrigerator, reaching into a cupboard for sugar. 'I'll find out what she did to him and let you know.'

'I'd rather you didn't.' Margaret was repressive.

'It's not good to let things fester. He should have confided in you.'

'Well, he didn't.'

'He should have.'

'Claud's business is Claud's business.'

'And you are not interested?'

Margaret shot a spiteful glance at her tormentor, poured her a mug of tea with a steady hand.

She'd like to throw the pot at me, thought Laura. 'You'll grow out of this,' she said and put two lumps of sugar into her mug, plop, plop.

'What do you mean?'

'You will grow out of wanting shot of Claud.' Laura stirred her tea.

'God!' said Margaret. 'I don't know what you are doing here. I didn't invite you. I don't know why you are interested in Claud—'

'He's pretty, he's intelligent—'

'You are old enough to be his mother—'

'Sure.'

'As his mother I have every right to let him lead his own life—'

'And not tangle with yours?' Laura's eyes sparkled with amusement. 'You want to live somewhere where you can twiddle the knobs of your own television, choose your own programmes, go to bed without the fear of being woken by Claud coming in drunk and being sick before he can reach the loo. You don't want to be bothered by his heart cracking about the place over some idiot girl. You are abdicating parenthood.'

'You have been spared parenthood,' said Margaret, 'you prying bitch.' She said in friendly accents, 'Tell me, was it your uncle who attacked Claud?'

'My uncle?'

'Nicholas.'

'Oh, Nicholas. I rarely think of him as my uncle. I couldn't think what you meant for a moment. Yes, it was. He was cross because I gave Claud junk from the attic. It was a mistake to tell them. I should just have helped myself, they would never have noticed. It was my innate honesty.'

Margaret sniffed.

'They are funny about possessions,' said Laura.

'They are funny full stop,' said Margaret. 'I've often heard their house referred to as the Funny Farm.' This was not true, but it pleased Margaret to say it. She found herself blaming Laura for Claud's drunkenness, his black eye, his being sick in the hall, none of which she had minded much at the time since, compared with her late husband's behaviour, it was mild stuff. 'If you are passing anywhere near Claud's loft would you drop some boxes of knick-knacks and china I've packed up for his stall?'

'All right, I'll go. I can take a hint,' said Laura, putting down her empty mug. 'Where are these boxes?' she asked, unruffled.

Neither woman spoke as they transferred the boxes of junk from the boot of Margaret's car to Laura's. Then Laura asked, 'Does Claud want you to leave the neighbourhood? Does he know you are going?'

'There is not room for both of us,' said Margaret.

'You do not mean you and Claud, do you? You mean you and me.'

Margaret smiled.

'I shall find out about that girl,' said Laura, getting into her car.

'Oh, that.' Margaret's smile broadened. 'She was just the beginning of the rapids.'

Laura started the engine, reached for her safety belt. 'I am not at all a maternal sort of friend,' she said.

'Who wants a maternal friend?' asked Margaret falsely.

'Claud? Perhaps Claud does.'

'He's not likely to find one, is he?' Margaret watched Laura go. I wonder what she's after, she thought. Then, turning back into the house, she thought, I can't help him. If I stayed on here, I wouldn't be of the slightest use to him, while Laura will believe in him, give him the courage to write his novel. The trouble with me, she thought honestly, is that I simply cannot believe in this wretched novel, I can't imagine Claud as a writer.

Standing at the sink, rinsing the mugs she and Laura had used, Margaret experienced the feeling of desolation that had assailed her on Claud's first day at school; there seemed little difference between Claud aged five and Claud aged twenty-three. His mix of boldness and timidity was unchanged. At five he had kicked her shins when thwarted, screamed for help if injured, twisted away from her. He had also come running for help and reassurance in time of trouble (he did not do that any more). He had expected her to be there if needed. I always was there, she thought as she dried the mugs and hung them on the dresser.

What am I worrying about? He's a grown man. She unhooked the mug Laura had used. Was there still sugar on the bottom? She rinsed the mug a second time.

Was that lipstick? She looked closely at the mug. She doesn't use lipstick, her mouth is naturally red. Will she and Claud—? Margaret stood holding the mug. I despise possessive mothers, she thought. If Laura should want him and he should want her?

There's nothing I can do, she thought. She shrugged her shoulders and replaced the mug on its hook.

Sly of her to find that packet of photos— It never occurred to me to look for— I defended him, didn't I? I stood up for his independence. Am I jealous? Of Laura? Why did Claud never talk to me about Amy, whoever she is? He never brought her home, Margaret thought resentfully. What am I fussing about? Until Laura came by I was planning to sell up and make my getaway.

Getaway, she thought, there's a word. Then she thought, Laura guessed it all, she understands what I am doing, that it's best for—

This train of thought was interrupted by the sound of Laura returning. Margaret went to the door; Laura leaned from the driver's seat. 'On second thoughts, Margaret, I don't really want that chest, is that all right?'

'Yes, of course. Thank you. Don't worry.' What am I thanking her for? 'Thanks,' she repeated. Laura drove away waving.

Closing the door Margaret smiled grimly. 'I am doing what is best for me,' she said out loud, 'as I intended before she interrupted me.' I am not letting Claud down, she told herself; I shall be on the telephone, should he want me.

Margaret snatched up the mug Laura had used and smashed it onto the floor, where it broke. Then, slightly shamefaced, she fetched a dustpan and brush and swept up the pieces and tipped them into the dustbin. Washing her hands under the tap, she found herself feeling grateful to Laura for inspiring this small rush of adrenalin.

Laura eased up the trap-door and moved a step higher up the ladder. From this position she could see Claud sitting stooped at the table, one hand clutching a piece of crushed typing paper, the other on his knee, fingers drumming. He did not notice her. He stared up through the attic window. She knew that all he could see from there was the sky, perhaps a gull wheeling past or a rapid flight of starlings; if he wished for a more interesting view, he would have to stand up (or look at me, she thought).

Claud dropped the crushed paper onto the floor, straightened his back, put a fresh sheet of paper in the machine and began to tap; she was interested to see that he appeared confident and resolute. She kept quiet while he chuntered along to the end of a paragraph, stopped, leaned forward to read what he had written, hissed through his teeth and resumed typing. The paper finished, he released it from the machine and, laying it on a pile of manuscript, inserted a fresh sheet and carried on. He kept this up for three more pages before coming to a halt. Then he whistled a shrill note of satisfaction and stood up, rubbing his hands together. As he pushed his chair back he caught sight of her head poking up through the trap-door level with the floor. He stared. Laura did not move.

'You look like someone in a Beckett play,' he said.

Laura smiled.

He thought perhaps her eyes were so bright because of the bluish tint of the whites, that he was pleased to see her, that he liked her pointed nose and the way her hair sprang back from her forehead. He thought she looked strange and exciting, that he was pleased, glad, he liked the way she was there not speaking.

He crossed the loft to the trap-door, knelt, then lay, his face on a level with hers. He said, 'I thought you had disappeared for good.'

'You did?'

'Where have you been?'

'London.'

'With that musician, the chap I saw you with at the concert? Is he your lover?'

'No.' (Not any more.)

'Ah.'

'Ah.'

'I have been thinking of you so much.' (That isn't true, but I should have been thinking of her, my word yes, I certainly should.) 'Missing you,' he said. Of course he'd missed her.

'And you? How goes the book? It's new, isn't it? You scrapped the two paras and sixteen sentences?'

'How did you guess? They were rubbish.'

'So this is about?'

Claud told her the schema, the character who might be his mother, her peculiar relationship with household machinery, lying on the floor propped on his elbows, his face level with hers. Her hair smelled exciting. It smelled of pepper. 'Shall you come up?' he asked.

'If you insist. I am quite comfortable here standing on the ladder, getting a mouse's eye view of your loft.'

'It is your loft. I am only here on sufferance.'

'Oh, no.' She stepped up the ladder. There had been a warm flow of air from the house below fanning up her skirt; she was reluctant to leave it for the austerity of the loft. 'Oh, you have a stove. What luxury.' She strolled about looking at Claud's things, his clothes hanging limp on nails, his books, the bed which had been hers many years ago. She looked out of the window and was reassured by the unchanged view; she touched the table, let a finger rest for a second on the manuscript, sat down on the bed. 'And who else? Who else is in your book?'

'Oh - I - er—'

'Well?' She was sharp.

Claud answered with a rush of words spewed out, speeded by emotion. 'There's a girl, she bloody intrudes, she's not supposed to be in it but she keeps bobbing up and I do-not-want-her.'

'Someone you were - or are - in love with?' Laura spoke lightly, looking away from him, giving him the chance to rat on the bitch. (In what way had she hurt him?)

'Well,' said Claud, off-hand, 'you know how it is, adolescent love, first love I suppose, the usual sort of nonsense. She recurs, that's all, a sort of emotional burp.'

'Much in love? It was heavy?'

'Oh God, yes, but I wouldn't give her a second thought now. She doesn't fit the scenario, that's what is so aggravating.'

'Sit here.' Laura patted the bed beside her.

'I mean,' said Claud, obeying, 'she played a small and unimportant rôle in my life, it was quite brief.' He spoke protestingly, wishing Amy had been small, unimportant.

'Brevity is neither here nor there. She is obviously someone who needs exorcising. What did she do to you?' Laura probed like a dentist at a raw nerve and leaned against Claud beside her on the bed.

He liked the way she smelled of pepper. He put his arm around her. 'You smell so—'

'So what?'

'Different.'

'From what?'

'Other people.'

'We all smell different. Now tell me about this

intruding girl. What was her name?'

'I'd rather not. She was called Amy.'

'Shall we take our clothes off and get into bed?'

'Take our clothes off?' Claud sat up straight.

'Yes.'

'Undress?' His voice rose in panic.

'Yes.'

'It's nearly lunch time.'

'I shall treat you as an *hors d'oeuvre*.'

Claud sprang off the bed, undressed, tearing off his clothes, his back modestly turned, his heart thumping in a mix of alarm and excitement. When he turned round Laura was in the bed between the sheets still wearing her sweater.

'You cheated.' He scrambled in beside her. His legs felt weak.

'Only my top half—'

'Oh.' She was right; below the waist she had no clothes on. 'Oh,' he muttered, 'Oh my G—'

'What was she like, this girl Amy?' asked Laura an hour later, when they had had a refreshing and recuperative nap.

Claud came down from cloud nine. 'Must you bring her up, the stupid bitch?'

'What did she do to you?' (The dentist's drill.)

Claud shouted: 'She would not take her Walkman off when we made love.'

Laura did not laugh. 'I can see that that was serious,' she said. (I've got the tooth out. God, how it must hurt.)

'You can?'

'Wounding.'

'It was.'

'Did she perform in time to the music?' (Just a little dab of antiseptic.)

'How would I know?'

'So you threw her out?'

'She threw me. It was her flat.'

'Worse.'

'Thanks for not laughing. I took a risk telling you.'

'You know, I think she fits in the novel. Your mother's machines, a Walkman, quite a small part of course.' (Now rinse and spit.)

'Do you really think so?'

'Definitely.'

'Okay, I'll let her in. I think you are right.'

'Good.' (Rinse just once more and spit again. In no time you will think you thought of this yourself.) The afternoon sun made a pool of light on the floor. Seagulls shrieked across the roofs, lorries passed grumbling up the street. 'Long ago,' said Laura, 'when I was young, I got stinking drunk at a party. In the morning when I woke I realised that someone had shared my bed.'

'He'd raped you?'

'I don't think it was rape.'

'Who was it?' Claud felt his throat constrict.

'There was this smell of hair oil on my pillow, nothing else.'

'Hair oil?'

'People used hair oil in those days, dumbo.'

'Of course.' He remembered his father using some sharp-smelling mix of oil and spirit. 'So?'

'So ever since I hope to recognise it on some stranger I may be introduced to.'

'But people don't use hair oil any more.'

'They don't, do they.'

'Did you make this up to make me feel comfortable after telling you about Amy?' Claud was suspicious.

'I wouldn't do a thing like that.'

But watching Laura dress Claud thought that's just what she would do.

'Come on,' said Laura, 'I'm starving. Let's get ourselves lunch, it's not too late.'

As he followed her down the ladder Claud felt a rush of gratitude. She had not embarrassed him by asking to read his manuscript. She had not mocked. He felt assuaged, relaxed, masculine and bouncy, positively confident. When she suggested lunching at the wine bar, he agreed. It would be nice, it would round off a successful morning to have Mavis unwrapped from her awful overcoat stand pliant by their table to take their order. 'Would it bore you to read my manuscript?' he asked with a generosity which he instantly regretted.

They were walking up the street leaning into a draughty wind. Laura did not answer immediately. She was thinking that it was one thing to possess Claud's body, there was much good work she could do there, but was she prepared to take on his mind? 'I would not be bored,' she said carefully, 'but wary. It's a big responsibility.'

Claud felt downcast; he wished he could retract his offer. It was not an offer he would have made to Mavis, for instance, or his mother or Amy, if they had still been on speaking terms. My work is private, he thought, his mind running already on a line roughly parallel to Laura's.

'I should be flattered,' said Laura, 'but think it over.'

'How civilised you are,' exclaimed Claud, relieved and ebullient. He pushed open the door of the wine bar. 'What shall we eat? Come on, let's sit here where we sat before. Let's harass Mavis.'

But Mavis was not there. Her place had been taken

by a gangling youth wearing a white apron stretching down to his feet, who looked at Claud with contempt. 'Didn't you know,' he said, as he looked forward to telling them that everything was off except yesterday's quiche, 'didn't you know that Mavis has got a part in a London show? She got a phone call last night and went off at the speed of light, borrowed the rail fare and hopped it. Right, then. You want to eat? Everything's off except the quiche. Might be able to rustle up some salad.'

'No matter,' said Laura, opening her bag and extracting her purse. 'Just take off that silly apron and streak down to the fishmonger's like a good boy, and bring back two dozen oysters. We will eat them with lots of brown bread and butter. Bring half a pound of prawns, too.'

'Nobody here can open oysters,' said the boy mutinously.

'But I can,' said Laura. 'Now scoot.'

'You bloody Thornbys,' said the boy, taking the money. 'Bloody, bloody people.'

'And bring an oyster knife and a lemon,' Laura called after him.

Mavis had arrived early for the train. The wind penetrated her thick coat as she waited for the signal to turn green. She had been foolish to leave home so soon; but she had been consumed by train fever, crazy to be on her way in the Inter-City train which would take her to London where some day, not immediately of course, her name would be up outside a theatre in electric glory.

Terrence had wanted to see her off – he was taking her place in the wine bar – but she had told him to be sure to get to work on time. 'Make yourself indispensable,' she had said. He would be there now, she thought pityingly, wearing the apron he had stolen for a joke from a café on the school trip to France the year before last.

Her mother had said: 'Why don't you ask Claud to see you off? He's only up there typing.' Poor old Mum would not understand that part of this joyous departure would be Claud's surprise when he heard that she had gone to work at her true vocation instead of eating her heart out taking orders from all those boring, barely literate vegetable growers, dull provincials who didn't know, wouldn't accept, that she was an actress. Had not Laura pointed her out to Claud in that joking way of hers which put one down? 'You wouldn't believe Mavis was an actress.' Something like that.

'Goodbye, goodbye,' hummed Mavis, pacing the platform, seventy paces to the end, seventy paces back. I have got it all together, she thought with satisfaction. And Claud, how surprised would he be? She had not told him. Nor had she told anyone, least of all her mother, the world's greatest blabbermouth in Mavis' opinion, that the part she had so joyfully accepted was that of understudy. Understudy to an extremely healthy little actress often boringly described by the agent they shared as 'a great little trouper'.

Mavis turned away from the wind. People were beginning to trickle onto the platform. Not too long now for the off.

I shan't get paid much, she thought, lucky I've saved. Pity I'm not a man, they sell their sperm to make ends meet - a curious piece of information from Terrence who had learned it from a programme on

TV. He had added nastily, 'Doesn't seem fair, does it, that girls have to prostitute,' using prostitute as a verb; he had always sat among the 'could-do-betters' at school.

Of course one had done jobs for Laura while at drama school, that was not prostitution. I am a virgin and wish to stay that way, Mavis chuckled, remembering Claud fumbling up from the waistband of her jeans, his hand trapped between vest and tee-shirt. 'And a virgin I will be,' Mavis hummed. Ah! The signal had turned green, cling cling went the telegraph. She could hear the train shriek on the far side of the hill as it plunged from the cutting into the hillside. If that's not sexual, I don't know what is, thought Mavis who, while avoiding personal experience, had read a lot of books. As she snatched up her bags in readiness for the train she felt a surge of excitement as sharp as sex. I shall not be an understudy for ever. She heaved her bags onto the rack. I am not mislaying my virginity. Oh no! she vowed as she settled into a corner seat, not if that's what it leads to, she thought, as her ears reacted to the screams of an infant across the aisle. Oh Jesus, no! she thought as the infant's sibling lost its footing and fell flat, its precarious balance faulted by the train jerking into motion. Claud is not all that attractive, she thought. All that can wait, what cannot wait is my career.

Mavis took cotton wool from her bag and stuffed bits into her ears, a practice she had learned when doing prep while her mother watched soaps on television. Settling in her seat, she stared out of the train window but she did not see the scenery flash by. She only saw herself and her future.

*   *   *

Claud watched Laura open the oysters; at any minute he expected the lethal knife to slip and her bright blood gush. Would it look like ketchup or blood orange juice as it dripped over the oysters? He had once watched a large red moon rise from a backdrop of oystershell cloud. 'Do be careful,' he said, appalled by the risks she was taking. The moonrise had presaged a violent storm.

Laura eased an oyster from its shell, pinched a drop of lemon juice onto it and handed it to Claud. 'Try that.'

Claud bit the oyster, swallowed. 'Heavenly.'

'Bread and butter, pot boy!' Laura shouted.

'Coming, you great bully.' The boy, who had resumed his apron, came rushing from the back of the wine bar, long strides threatening to trip him. He carried aloft a dish of brown bread generously buttered.

They had the bar to themselves, all other lunchers having long gone. 'What's your name, pot boy?' Laura offered the boy an oyster. 'Like one?'

'Yes, please.' The boy swallowed the oyster. 'The name's Terrence, not Terry. Thanks.' His Adam's apple wobbled in his thin throat. 'Looks like you've forgotten me,' he said. 'I'm the boy you used for that experiment, remember, plaster cast it was.'

'Oh!' Laura laughed. 'Of course I remember you, you were a wicked little nipper.'

Laura and the boy laughed together, excluding Claud from some mystifying intimacy.

'If you'd like to run and get some more oysters,' she said, 'you can join our feast. I'm feeling rich today.'

'I certainly would,' said the boy. 'You two celebrating something?' He looked sly, his eye resting on Claud.

'Possibly,' said Laura, pausing from her work to take money from her bag. 'If you run like the clappers, I shall have half a dozen ready for you when you get back.'

'Okay,' said Terrence, and ran, letting the wine bar door slam.

'You have amazingly strong hands,' said Claud. Aware that the hands he watched had recently caressed him, he felt a prick of reminiscent desire in recollection of their tenderness. They were not being tender to the oysters.

'It's my work.'

'Your work? What work?'

'I don't just fan about doing nothing,' said Laura.

'What at? Doing what?'

'I have a business in London.'

Terrence, returning with a fresh batch of oysters, put paid to further enquiry.

'How is your um—' asked the boy and prolonged his hesitation.

'My what?' Laura looked up at the boy.

'Mr Thornby.' Terrence glanced at Claud. 'Mr Nicholas Thornby,' he smirked.

'Fine, thanks,' Laura answered. 'He's busy, he works for several papers now.'

'Doing what?' asked Claud.

'He writes articles, reviews books, does travel stuff, that sort of thing. He and my mother work as a team.'

'I see.' Claud watched Laura and the boy arranging the oysters on plates, alternating the oysters with rosy prawns and quarters of lemons.

'And does your – um – er – still help with your work?' asked Terrence, licking salt from his fingers. 'The old man.' There was a subterranean impertinence in the enquiry which Claud found disturbing.

'He never did.' Laura was brusque. 'We lead separate lives,' she said, concentrating on a prawn she was peeling.

'Who is, what is, who does he mean by er, and um? What's the mystery?' Claud was irritated by the intimacy which, springing from nowhere between Laura and Terrence, excluded him.

'One can see you haven't had your ear to the ground when you've been at home,' said Terrence perkily. 'Why, even your mum would know what and who I am talking about.' He bit a prawn, crunching it shell and all between large teeth.

'Don't choke on its whiskers,' said Laura equably. 'What the little sod is hinting at, Claud, is that there's a legend in these parts that my uncle Nicholas is also my father.'

Claud gaped.

'It's general knowledge,' said Terrence, pouring an oyster into his mouth.

Claud watched the boy's Adam's apple rise and fall. He tried to find something to say and failed.

'It tightens the familial bonds,' said Terrence. 'These oysters are delish. Everybody knows about the Thornby family.'

'Everybody knows the moon is made of Stilton cheese,' said Laura. 'Eat some bread and butter with your oysters, Terry.'

'Terrence,' said Terrence.

'Brought you each a glass of stout, that's what you need with that lot.' The owner of the wine bar appeared from the back premises with a tray. Laura smiled up at him as he set the glasses on the table. 'On me,' he said, returning her smile. 'Don't stick around here, boy, there's plenty for you to do at back.' He looked at Terrence without affection, turned and went away.

'Thank you,' Laura called after him. 'Great!'

'Who invented this libel?' asked Claud, recapturing his cool.

'It's just something I grew up with,' said Laura, 'a wartime legend. Nicholas and Emily found it amusing.'

'Mr Thornby finds lots of things amusing, doesn't he?' said Terrence. 'Hey! He didn't bring me any stout! I seem to remember Mr Nicholas found your work pretty comical.'

'What is your work?' asked Claud, beginning to find Terrence's gnatlike presence a trial. 'Do tell me if it's not a secret.'

'There's no secret. I do restoration work.'

'Oh,' said Claud, 'I see. What do you restore?'

'She makes new noses and fingers for classical statues,' said Terrence. 'Noses, fingers and cocks, all the things iconoclasts knock off.'

'Fancy you remembering such a long word,' said Laura, peeling another prawn.

'She makes models from life with plaster casts,' said Terrence. 'She had me standing in for a putto when I was small, that was a laugh. My mum supposed Mr Nicholas stood in for the mature male statues. She's got a comical mind, my ma.'

'Terry, come and clear up back here,' came a stentorian voice from behind the bar.

'Dear, dear, must go, thanks for the nosh.' Terrence gulped his last oyster and scuttled away.

'What a horrible boy,' exclaimed Claud. 'Did you really? I mean did he – oh, Lord.'

'Are you shocked?' Laura drank deep of her stout. 'Delicious Guinness, so good for me.'

'Of course not. Yes. No. It seems a bit odd. How did you - er - manage?'

Laura was laughing. 'Oh, Claud, you are shocked. Terrence is a mythomaniac, every town has one. Eat your oysters before they die.' Claud obeyed, scoffing his last two oysters, tasting only the salt. 'It's extremely difficult,' Laura was saying, 'to make a cast of a child's nose, you have to plug its nostrils and bloody little Terry kept sneezing.'

'Nose?' exclaimed Claud. 'I thought you meant, I thought he meant—'

'Cocks?' Laura was really laughing now. 'Oh, Claud, you are gullible.'

Claud did not enjoy being mocked. 'Why,' he asked, deflecting the subject, 'did your uncle, your father, put a bucket over my head and knock me downstairs?'

'Still harping on that! What a worrying bulldog it is. Nicholas and Emily thought I was giving you treasures from the attic. It's piled high with stuff they don't like or need but cannot bear to part with. Do we have to go on about this?'

'No, no. I'm sorry I brought it up.'

They finished the prawns and bread and butter, drank their stout. Watching the rim of froth on his glass Claud remembered his terror. When drunk he had thought he saw Laura in triplicate, she had looked so peculiar flanked by Nicholas and Emily, so unlike the woman who now sat beside him, who a short while ago had lain in his arms. 'They are your *doppelgängers*,' he said.

'No,' said Laura sharply. 'We are all real, we are each separate. If they make you uneasy, find them a place in your novel.'

'Wouldn't you mind?'

'Why should I? They will not be recognisable.'

'In that case I'll bear them in mind,' said Claud. 'One rather good idea would be to insert bloody Amy and her Walkman, don't you think? I think she will fit in nicely.' (Already my suggestion is his inspiration. Laura applauded herself.) 'Amy might match up rather well with your mythomaniac, what is his name?'

'Terrence,' said Laura.

'Oh, Laura, I love you,' said Claud, delighted.

'Oysters are supposed to be aphrodisiac.' Laura piled the empty shells into a pyramid.

'I mean I love you. Love. Love, not to be confused with lust.'

'No?'

'Though of course love and lust are synonymous.'

'Like oil and vinegar in mayonnaise?'

'You bring me to earth,' Claud cried.

'Was Amy a successful mayonnaise?' asked Laura lightly.

'No,' exclaimed Claud, 'she curdled. I must have been a poor cook.'

(Little does the poor boy know, thought Laura.)

'Of course you weren't,' she said. You will be very good indeed before I finish with you, she thought with amusement. 'Come on, Otis,' she said, 'I must go.'

'Why Otis?' Claud helped her into her coat. 'You called me Otis when I met you in the market. Why Otis?'

'It's just a name I like, a private joke. Otis reminds me of lifts, lifts go up and down. When I first saw you I thought you had spirit which might go up and down. Otis,' said Laura, 'in case you've never noticed, is a maker's name, you see it on lifts. Am I being pedantic?'

'Not at all,' said Claud, at last latching on. 'My spirits are high, they swoop.'

'Up, up and away.' Laura kissed his cheek and was off down the street in a rush.

PART II

Winter

By vanishing to London Mavis created a vacuum in the Kennedy household. Without her daughter Ann Kennedy became depressed. She went to bed late, got up later still, wasted hours slumped in front of the television. 'I know we argued,' she said to Claud, catching him on his way upstairs. 'We used to spar quite a bit, it kept us on our toes. Now look at me, I am collapsing into old age without Mavis to goad me along.'

'I wouldn't say that, Mrs Kennedy, I wouldn't call it collapse.' Claud fidgeted, anxious to reach his typewriter and note down an idea for his current chapter before he lost it.

'Call me Ann, you've been in the loft long enough to call me Ann. You can't deny the old age bit. Guess how old I am.'

Claud thought he was too wise to guess; Ann Kennedy looked as old as his mother on a bad day, every day. 'Okay, Ann, thanks. It's not old age. You are lonely, that's all. It's natural to miss her, she's your only child.'

'Does your mother miss you?'

'Not so you'd notice. I wouldn't know.'

'Thought not. Would you like me to cook you your breakfast now Mavis is gone? It must cost you quite a bit going to the wine bar every morning.'

'I quite like the wine bar.' His privacy threatened, Claud stiffened.

'With Mavis gone? It would be no trouble to get your breakfast.'

My God, she thinks I go to the wine bar because of Mavis. How crazy, she obviously doesn't connect me with Laura.

'I thought you went to the wine bar so you could watch Mavis looking pretty in her overall and have her take your order and say, Yes, sir and no, sir.'

'She never said Yes, sir and no, sir. She was inclined to be bossy and hurry one up so that someone else could have the table.'

'Oh, really?' Mrs Kennedy took this as an insult. 'Bossy, was she? That's not what other people say—'

'Not bossy in any derogatory sense, Mrs Kennedy.'

'Ann. There only is a derogatory sense to bossy, quote me another—'

'All right. Ann. She was bossy in a rather jolly and amusing way. The customers, as you say, liked it.' (If she doesn't let me get to my manuscript, I shall hit her.)

'The customers were mostly her friends, they would like it.'

'Mrs Kennedy, Ann, I've put my foot in it. I have ruffled you,' he apologised.

'I'm not ruffled, I just said—'

'I found Mavis lovely, a stunner.' Claud raised his voice, 'She was pliant and appealing in her overall and I do assure you pretty, no, not pretty, absolutely competent as well.' Claud moved towards the door; they had been standing in the kitchen. Mrs Kennedy barred his way to the stairs.

'Oh.'

'I had no intention of insulting Mavis or hurting your maternal feelings. I—'

'That's all right, then. I just thought—'

'It was nice of course to see her in her overall, not totally concealed by that enormous overcoat,' Claud carried on, realising as he spoke that he carried on too far. He shifted his weight onto his right foot as though about to walk through Ann Kennedy.

'It's a very good coat, it's the fashion to wear very large coats.'

'I know, I read about it somewhere.'

'A girl like Mavis, an actress, has to be à la mode—'

'Ann.' If only she would let him get by, get to the stairs, get to work. 'Ann.'

'Yes?'

'Don't get carried away.'

'I do get carried away. I lie awake nights expecting to hear that she's been raped on her way to rehearsal. London is dangerous.'

'More likely on the way back, and she could equally well get herself raped here.' The conversation was bolting along a fresh avenue. 'I myself was tempted more than once.' (Beware of verbal diarrhoea.)

'Am I harbouring a rapist?'

'Only joking, Mrs Kennedy, Ann.'

'So I should hope. Now, what about your breakfast? Shall I or shall I not cook it?'

A compromise was reached: she would provide breakfast on Sundays when the wine bar was closed and on market days, since it was only sensible to brave the elements on a full stomach. Claud was to pay for these meals, he discovered later, by listening to dissertations on Mavis pram-bound, Mavis as a toddler, at primary school, at comprehensive and at drama school. As he ate his bacon and egg, grilled mushrooms with kidney and tomato, he learned to say, 'Oh, really', 'That was nice', 'She wasn't stupid, was she', and other such platitudes, while his mind plotted his next chapter, the few sheets of typescript which would increase the pile on his desk.

Some thousands of words later, reading through his work, Claud recognised a minor character taking on the hue of Mrs Kennedy and that the character who had imposed herself as Amy had chameleon-like transformed into an etherealised person with Mavis' face and Laura's body. The characteristics which had been loathsome in Amy were in this paper version funny, sexy and beguiling; he was creating someone he dreamed of at night, confusing her with Laura wearing her jersey and nothing else. He would wake with a shock and an erection and sniff the cold air of the loft for the elusive scent of pepper.

So too his mother, the woman who had chivvied him through childhood, wiped his snot, ironed his shirts and simultaneously endured the vagaries of his violent alcoholic father, changed as he tapped the keys of his typewriter; the real Margaret Bannister disappeared just as in reality she had retreated from the neighbourhood and his immediate life by selling her house and moving elsewhere. So smoothly did she leave that Claud, passing his old home a week after her going, found himself querying whether he had ever lived in it.

He stood in the road staring at the house, noting the small changes already effected by the new owner. His parents' curtains still hung inside the windows, but tied back; there was a new knocker out of proportion with the size of the door; the new owner had whitened the grey slate step; a white cat stared bleakly from beside the scraper, freshly painted black, no longer coated with clods of mud from his mother's gardening clogs. Standing in the road he expected his mother to come round the house carrying the trug which held her fork and trowel, the garden gloves she never remembered to wear; she would be followed by her striped cat who lived under the delusion that it was a dog.

The door opened suddenly and a stranger stood in the doorway. The white cat nipped past her into the house. The woman spoke, articulating clearly. 'Can I help you?' (She was grey, one of the grey people.)

Claud became aware that she was nervous, that his mother's cat had been dead some years, that perhaps the picture he had seen in his mind's eye might never have existed. 'I am just casing the joint,' he said angrily.

The new owner shut the door smartly in his face. Perhaps she would telephone the police? Claud fished in his pocket for a pencil and the notebook in which he jotted escaping ideas. He wrote: 'I am only Claud Bannister, the erratic son of the previous owner, no need to panic.' He pushed the note through the letterbox. The letterbox snapped at his fingers; it was new, like the knocker. His parents' letterbox had had a weak spring, it got stuck open letting in unnecessary draughts in cold weather. He was assailed by sadness, felt fierce pangs of remorse. He had so often been beastly to his mother. He shouted: 'Fuck you, go to hell,' bending down and yelling through the letterbox. It nipped his fingers again; he turned and ran, racing down the road to take shelter in the nearest public house.

He went to bed that night rather drunk and dreamed of a procession of women, none of whom were exactly his mother or Amy or Mavis; his dream turned to nightmare as the woman clasped in his arms turned into Ann

Kennedy: 'Christ, what are you doing in my bed?' He woke trembling, sniffed, smelled pepper. 'Laura?'

'Yes.'

'Where have you been?'

'London. You were dreaming.'

'Nightmare – my mother – then I thought I was in bed with Ann Kennedy.'

'Oh dear!'

'Is it really you?' He was fully awake now.

'Yes.'

'What are you doing here?'

'Try and guess.'

'I often wake and you are not there.'

'How is Amy? Amy with her Walkman?'

'Changed, she's quite a raver now, marvellous, kind – gentle too.'

'On paper.'

'Yes, on paper, of course she's on paper.'

'What power you have.'

'On paper. How long have you been away?'

'I don't know. A few days.'

'How long are you back for?'

'I don't know.'

'Laura.'

'Yes.'

'The people in my book are more real than you and me, Brian and Susie, my mother or the market people.'

'So?'

'D'you think I'm going mad?' he whispered.

'I think you are becoming a writer.'

'You're not joking?'

'I'm not joking.'

'My God.' Claud lay back on the bed. 'Gosh,' he said. 'Oh my goodness gracious me, oh my holy heavens.'

Laura sniffed.

'You sniffed? Laura, what is it?'

'If you'd leave your book for a moment or two I'd show you.'

In Claud's arms Laura sensed a change; he had grown older, more certain, he had matured. It was not a simple matter of a better turn of love-making and good timing. There was a passion and tenderness he had not shown before. She was, while finding this matching delightful and enjoyable, also puzzled. Then she realised with shock what was happening: he was making love not to her, but to this girl he had invented. She gave Claud's neck a sharp nip.

He cried out, 'What's that for?' and sprang apart from her.

'Isn't it about time you let me read your manuscript?'

'I am afraid to.' He swung his legs off the bed and sat with his back turned to her.

'You are presumably writing a book which you expect will eventually be published?'

'Of course.'

'And people will read it?'

'Faceless people, people I do not know or care for.'

'Your friends will read it, they too are the public.'

'I had not thought. Do you want to read it?'

'Yes.'

Claud stood up, picked his shirt off the floor, put it on and went to stand looking out across the roofs to the river. 'People are right when they talk of the cold light of dawn. I am full of trepidation,' he said. He took the manuscript from the table and laid it in Laura's lap.'Nobody has seen this,' he said as he switched on the bedside lamp so that she could see to read. 'I suppose I can trust you to tell me the truth.'

'Yes.' How easily one said yes.

He tapped the typescript. 'These are my guts.'

'Oh,' said Laura, 'guts.'

'If this book is not well received, if it fails, well, to you it may sound silly, but the truth is I shall kill myself.'

'*Feel* like killing yourself.'

'No, I shall actually do it.'

Laura said: 'Oh *hell*.' Setting out to be amused, she had become interested, more interested than was safe. Claud was not like Clug, he would not be going back to Roumania next week.

Claud was speaking. 'It's very difficult to explain, Laura darling' (he had not called her darling before) 'but it's intense. The people in this book are real. The girl is as real as you, she has your legs for a start, your lovely legs, I love her – no, I can't explain—'

'I think,' Laura said, 'that I had better not read this.' She took the typescript and held it out to him. 'Anyway, I should not read it until it is finished.'

'Okay.' He took the manuscript and laid it back in its place on the table. 'All right,' he said, 'I understand. But I meant what I said. I—'

'Yes,' said Laura. Then, 'Why don't we resume what we were at when I bit you?'

'Oh, Laura—'

'Only this time make love to me not to Amy.'

'She's not called Amy any more.'

'Well, just concentrate on fucking me. I don't like acting proxy. I'm no good at it.'

'All right, Laura, I shall enjoy that.' Claud got back into bed. 'And later, when it's day, we could have breakfast in the wine bar,' he said.

'Stop talking,' she said.

* * *

'Can we talk now?' Claud asked presently.

'What about?' Laura stared at the dark oblong of the uncurtained window. 'Your book?'

'No, you. I want to know all about you.'

Laura said nothing.

'Tell me what you did when you had this loft. Did you bring lovers here?'

'I told you. I came here to be private. Ann's husband was alive in those days. A nice man, sensitive. He understood my need to be alone. I bet Ann misses him.'

'I don't want to talk about Ann. Tell me about your lovers, I won't be jealous.' But Claud felt a rush of jealousy. Had she in this bed done to others what she— 'Please tell me, I need to know.'

'You need to know!' Laura leaned back, her head on her arms.

'When people fall in love they tell each other everything,' said Claud.

Laura laughed. 'The more fools they.'

'Don't mock. Who did you bring up here? I think I am a bit jealous. Not Brian?' (Susie's Brian, he felt quite hot at the idea.)

'Not Brian,' Laura answered gravely.

'Sorry. I am jealous. I admit it.'

'A boring unprofitable emotion.'

'Who did you bring up here?' He leaned over, his mouth against hers, kissing urgent, questioning kisses.

Christopher had not kissed like this that one time she had allowed him up here. He had not been a fast learner like Claud. Laura kissed Claud back. 'That's nice,' she said. 'Very nice.'

'Not boring?' He leaned over her smiling.

'Not at all.'

'So who did you bring here? Who lay with you in this bed?' He watched her, trying to read the thoughts behind her eyes, very black in the pre-dawn light.

'Nobody.' She remembered Christopher on that wet and stormy afternoon in their teens when she had let him come here to her secret place and they had, for the first time, experimented with sex. She had not let him come again; his presence had disrupted her privacy. He had denigrated the loft. Instead, they had rolled about in his bed when his parents were out and he had declared himself 'in love'. Great fun was had for a time by both, she remembered, until – until what? For the life of her she could not remember what snide remark, spoken by whom, had caused her brain to click and realise that quite a lot of people believed that she and Christopher were brother and sister and that subtly, by not denying, Emily encouraged the idea.

Looking at Laura, seeing her frown, Claud tried to guess what went on behind those eyes. Laura was not thinking of him. He felt anxious, excluded.

Then her mother's complex relationship with Christopher's father had entered a new dimension. She knew then, she thought, why Ned paid her school bills. It was not goodness of heart, but a guilty response to blackmail. Why else should he have forked out for an expensive education at Cheltenham Ladies College, and a whole lot more? As she had often done since, Laura found herself admiring her mother's effrontery, her unorthodox method of raising funds for her daughter's education. But at the time, recoiling priggishly from what she thought she saw, she had choked Christopher off, brutally telling him that any warmth she felt for him would freeze to hate if bound by marriage.

Remembering the scene Laura smiled and Claud, watching, wondered.

Christopher, in the heat of first love, imagined in his innocence that love entailed marriage. He had been hurt, angry, refused to accept, become boring, and she had grown mocking, distant and in her turn cross. For not having been in love with him, she felt guilty.

Then in a rage she confronted her mother, and Emily laughed. Thirty years on Laura could hear that laugh. Emily had laughed from relief.

'What a bitch,' Laura muttered. Claud strained to hear, but could not.

Suspicious now, she had become aware of a groundswell of gossip. Whispers, suggestive wagers as to her provenance, and it was not Ned Peel who was hinted at, but Nicholas.

Laura closed her eyes and drew a long breath, as Claud watched.

She had not this time confronted her mother; she had come here to the loft where she had lain for twenty-four hours, weighting the trap-door with heavy books against intruders. Then, driven down by hunger, she had snatched a sandwich in Ann's kitchen before setting off across the fields to the Peels' house where she had asked Christopher's mother to lend her money. Rose Peel had refused to lend, but had given her five hundred pounds, asked no questions, tendered no advice.

Laura smiled in recollection. She had respected the older woman. Claud longed to know why she smiled, dared not interrupt.

She had cashed the cheque, packed a small bag, and set off abroad, hitching lifts, working her way across Europe, washing dishes or working at au pair jobs until she found herself working for a potter in Provence who taught her her trade.

For several years she had remained in a state of bellicosity and resentment against Nicholas and Emily; it waned as she returned to England, visited her mother and was made as welcome as though she had only been absent for a week. Emily had been charming, Nicholas too; she began to wonder whether she had misjudged them. She even went through a phase of suspecting Ned Peel again. Perhaps Rose Peel had not been so remarkable? She would have been glad to give the money, she would not want her only son to marry his half-sister. She might even, when she gave her the cheque, have thought she needed it for an abortion. Rose would not have wanted that sort of grandchild. She had juggled many mad suppositions rather than face the truth.

Then with acceptance came resignation tinged with hilarity, a philosophy, a mode of survival. There could be no marriage, no great love, no children, but plenty of friendship, good sex and always short-term relationships. Since it was quite difficult to find lovers to fit these criteria, there had not been many. Clug had been the latest.

Then what am I doing? Laura sat up and drew away from Claud. What a crazy idea to seduce Claud and install him in my loft. I must be mad. Here is somebody who breaks all my rules; he could become a lasting responsibility. What a dangerous aberration from my norm.

'I am sorry I nipped you,' she said.

Claud had forgotten the nip: 'Were you counting your lovers? You smiled.'

'My list is pretty sparse.' Laura got out of bed and began to dress, excluding Claud as she muffled her body. He would do better sticking to Amy, she thought, and chuckled.

'What's funny?' Claud cried angrily.

'I had a virtuous thought. Come on, get up, when I feel virtuous I feel hungry. Let's go and eat a hearty breakfast.' She hustled into her clothes, pulled on her boots. 'I crave hot coffee and croissants.'

Sulkily Claud reached for his pants. 'I crave you,' he said.

'Brian built those shelves for me,' said Laura, more to annoy herself than Claud. Brian had made a clumsy pass easily parried.

Claud did not rise to this, but with one leg in his trousers hopped to his work table to make a note; he had been seized with an idea, must note it down.

How soon will he bore me? Laura wondered, watching him. 'My threshold of boredom is a matter of weeks,' she said, but Claud was absorbed and did not hear.

Laura moved to the window and pressed her nose to the cold glass, then blew, steaming it up. She wrote: Christopher, Miklos the painter, Tony from the US, Clug, Claud. She rubbed at the names with her palm. 'It's cold out there,' she said. 'Very cold.'

Claud said, 'Um,' still writing.

Laura clenched her fists, blew again on the pane, clouding it, cutting out the view. 'There is no view,' she said. 'No view.'

Claud murmured. 'Um, just a minute,' writing with one hand, drawing his trousers on with the other.

I'd better get the view in proportion, Laura scolded herself. Time is up! He is becoming more than a toy boy, I have not been careful. 'Time is up,' she said out loud.

'Nearly finished,' said Claud, referring to his notes,

as he tucked in his shirt and pulled up his zip.

Laura watched. Thank God, she thought, he does not know that I have come whizzing down from London several times and not let him know. Twice I have watched him asleep and not got into bed with him; another time I drove away without coming into the house, but last night I weakened, was unwary, lost control.

She watched Claud. His features would coarsen, she thought, his looks would improve. A few lines across his forehead and from nose to chin would add interest to the too young face, add beauty. 'Oh, come on, Claud,' she said impatiently. 'Buck up.'

Claud threw down his pencil. 'You sound just like my mother,' he said. 'What have you written on the window?' He put his arms round Laura, pinning her arms to her sides, leaning over her shoulder, trying to decipher what she had written. 'A list of your lovers? Let me see, don't move.' Laura kept quite still, very still. 'Oh, darling, I wish you were like my mother, then I would not be jealous. I am so jealous.'

'Put it in your book. Use it.'

'I shall. My God, Laura.' He blew gently on the window pane. 'You have written my name. Look, it says Claud. As if I belonged to a list. What does it mean?' But Laura had ducked out of his arms and made for the ladder.

Margaret Bannister was happy in her new house; there was something astringent about its plain walls, an innocence of atmosphere which pleased. Whoever had lived in the house before her had left no trace.

As she arranged furniture and books, chose curtains, planned the garden, discovered her new village, made cautious friends with neighbours, her spirits rose. She felt an almost unholy glee at having distanced herself from Claud, and with Claud his father, whose memory lurked in the old house riddling her with guilt.

In this new ambience there was little to remind her of Claud or his father. In the old house she had been constantly reminded of scenes she would rather forget.

Open the kitchen cupboard and the door would stick where her husband had torn it off its hinge; in the bathroom was a crack in the mirror where he had hurled a toothglass. Every time she went into the garage she remembered the blow which had blacked her eye. In the bedroom she had too often lain wakeful, wondering what mood to expect when he returned, if he returned, for frequently he did not (I was held up). Long after their separation and his death she had remained uneasy. It was unfair to Claud to associate him with the fears, resentments and pains of her marriage, but she had done so. Now, splendidly free of inhibiting memories, she was free to love Claud without guilt, and remember his father with tenderness for the times of happiness and laughter – for they had shared happiness and enjoyed much laughter before she had developed an exaggerated fear of what she secretly thought of as 'the return from the pub'. By moving house she had cured the phobia.

As she arranged her kitchen cupboards Margaret dwelt on the good times, recovered her balance. She wished she had moved sooner.

Soon she would be ready to ask Claud to a meal, treat with him on her own terms minus the ghost of his father and the tiresomeness of his childhood, during which she suspected she had been too passive. Doormats make poor mothers, she told herself.

From the safe distance of thirty miles, she thought, without fussing, about Claud's chances of succeeding as a writer, wondered whether he had talent. She was glad that he had the market stall and inclined to put her money on that rather than what seemed to her an ephemeral novel. His writing craze might not last. She was grudgingly grateful to Laura for suggesting the stall; neither Claud nor herself would have had such a simple and original idea.

Before going to sleep – sleep was no problem in the new house – Margaret wondered what it might be like for Laura to have such a young lover and was surprised to find herself envying Laura's enterprise. She knew her husband would have enjoyed a Laura/Claud combination and this increased her fondness for his memory, eased the nagging sense of responsibility for his fatal coronary.

She remembered him an impulsive man. On impulse he had bashed the cupboard, thrown the toothglass, blacked her eye, threatened suicide, walked out on her. But she would not think of all that, rather remember the time he rushed her off to Paris for a lovely week in spring (fly now, pay later), bought her a dress he could not possibly afford, lured her into bed when they should have gone to a stuffy party.

A pity in a way that Claud was not like that, superficially yes, but not really. Claud's father would have made the running, not Laura.

Is there any running? How can I know? I must get another cat, she thought. I am too cautious to take a lover. Then she thought, What about Mavis, so pretty and presumably available? No, no, not with Laura around the horizon. She felt calm about Claud. Now that they were distanced she would not know if he got drunk or came a cropper. She would help by loving him, which cost nothing, and post the odd cheque to Ann Kennedy to subsidise the rent when she could afford it.

She bought a new frame for a snap of her husband taken by a crony, propping the bar of his favourite hostelry, and a matching frame for the snap of Claud taken by Amy whom she had never met, Amy who had made him so unhappy. Father and son were superficially alike. Claud's jaw was more determined, his smile less humorous. Were they really alike? She thought not. In habit, yes. Claud aped his father's trick of pissing out of windows when too lazy to go to the bathroom and she had recently seen him drunk, but that surely was exceptional.

What would he be like as a lover? Presumably he had muffed it with Amy; with Laura sex would be something else again, and any junketing with Mavis would be a repetition of Amy.

When I am completely settled, Margaret thought, I shall ask Claud over to see the house, observe what changes independence and his new career have made. It is weeks, months even, since I left.

Needing exercise Margaret set out for the shops. She would make enquiries about a kitten, have her sleeping pill prescription made up in case she reverted to insomnia, buy whisky to offer, should whisky drinkers call. So far only sherry drinkers had put their foot in the door, hopeful members of the WI which she had no intention of joining. Her husband had maintained that sherry drinkers always called first, true boozers later.

She was surprised, rounding a corner of the lane which led to the village, when an old man she had seen passing the plate in church stepped from behind a tree, opened his fly and exposed his large but drooping organ. Swerving so that her shopping basket knocked her knee Margaret walked on.

Should she have said Good afternoon? Nice day, isn't it? Asked whether he knew of a suitable kitten? Should she have said anything? To say nothing seemed so rude. Had she really seen what she thought she had seen?

In the supermarket she filled her basket with groceries, took two bottles of whisky from the shelf, paid at the check-out. He probably did it to everybody. It might be part of village life, something everyone knew about. She didn't want the village saying, 'That new woman at the White House is making trouble.' He passed the plate very nicely in church, waited for people to fumble for change.

She couldn't mention her encounter in the chemist, where the girl in the white uniform looked young and lofty as she took the prescription. 'Will you come back for it or wait? It will be ten minutes.'

'I'll wait.' There was a notice-board with lists of forthcoming events neatly pinned. Lists of lectures and films. Curious, thought Margaret, staring at the board, I have never except for my husband and Claud seen a man's penis. Claud had the neatest little thing as a baby, rather like an acorn.

'Mrs Bannister,' called the girl in the overall, 'your prescription.'

Margaret paid. 'I don't really need these,' she said. The girl looked down her nose. Outside the shop Margaret bumped into Claud.

'Claud!' She was joyously surprised. They hugged.

'Mother! I thought I saw you in there. Let me take your shopping.'

'I was going to invite you over when I got straight.'

'So you don't want to see me? It's weeks, months—'

'Is it? Time goes so – of course I want to see you. I didn't want to interrupt your work,' she lied.

'I'm taking an hour or two off. I thought I'd visit your new palazzo. This is jolly heavy. Buying booze now, that's not like you.'

'In case of visitors. Would you like a bottle to take back?'

'Thanks, I would. I'll hoard it for a future celebration. Look, I've borrowed Ann Kennedy's car. I'll drive you home.' He put the basket on the back seat, first taking one of the bottles and propping it in a corner. 'Get in, here we go! Which way now?'

'Turn right here and down that lane.' The old man had disappeared. Should she tell Claud? He had not been circumcised, she had noticed that; both Claud and his father were. 'One lives and learns,' she said.

'Learns what?' Claud changed gear.

'That's the house there, on the left,' she said. She would say nothing. She did not wish to appear inexperienced and naïve. It was wonderful to see Claud. 'I've missed you,' she said, which was partly true. 'This is an enterprising neighbourhood,' she said. 'There is a whole range of classes and lectures one can join: ecology, sociology, psychology, literature, art, archaeology – I was reading the list in the chemist.'

'Which will you take up?'

'I thought psychology would help me most.' Claud laughed. In the old days she might have felt diminished. 'No need to mock,' she said. 'Here we are. This is the house. Let me see what I can give you for lunch.'

'Anything will do.' He wished he had given her warning, she was such a good cook; living alone she probably didn't bother much. 'What an agreeable kitchen,' he said. 'Shall I put your shopping away?'

'Thank you.'

'I took you at your word about the whisky.'

'I meant you to. What about a risotto?'

'Delicious.' He was relieved.

While Margaret prepared the risotto, Claud explored the house. He had been miffed when she moved so suddenly, chose a house without consulting him, left him to come and find her; it did not fit the picture he had composed for himself of a tiresomely possessive parent. She had lived here solo, perfectly happy, for several months. As he went from room to room, finding familiar furniture in new poses, he began to rearrange his picture of his parent. Peering at the newly framed photographs of himself and his father he questioned rather uncomfortably whether he had not perhaps joined his father as a figure from his mother's past? Been cast off?

He shed this discomfort at lunch. While his mother talked about her new neighbourhood, the charms and conveniences of the village, he described the small triumphs of his stall. His book, he told her, was progressing. He was grateful, he said, for the money she sent Ann. Could she afford it? Should he not be independent?

'I like to help if I can,' she said. She was pleasurably surprised talking to him. He did not contradict, as he always had on principle, or smack her down when she ventured a political opinion contrary to his own. He was grown more civilised. He even laughed at her jokes. I shall not spoil this by mentioning Laura, she thought. She was reminded of the happier times with her husband.

Tucking into the risotto, salad, fruit, cheese and

excellent coffee, Claud forgave his parent her defection. Why should she not live where she pleased? If he made an effort, he could reach her here. He would not stay too long, though, in case the conversation slipped into the personal; she might link him with Mavis or make some reference to Amy. He could not possibly tell her that Amy was transformed into someone quite else. As he listened to his mother the part of his mind which concentrated on his novel began to question whether there were not parts of it mulched with sentimentality. What was it about his mother made him think this? She was having an effect similar to Laura's. Not, of course, the Laura in bed, there was no way he could imagine his mother making use of her legs as Laura did.

Margaret saw Claud smile, did not ask what the joke might be; she was happy that their shaky relationship was improved. She thought enviously of other parents who had secure relationships with their young, a constant exchange of confidences. As they talked she was content to remain in the shallows. It was quite amusing not to ask about Laura, to listen to Claud being cocky and adult, not quite as in love with himself as he had been. She did not, when it was time to go, press him to stay. She watched him drive away, waved at the departing car and as she did so remembered the old man in the lane, poor pitiful creature, and was curiously reminded of Claud newborn, a red and skinny infant, shaken by screams, his balls huge, out of all proportion to his size. She decided to put a pound in the collection next time she went to church and forget the incident in the lane.

She was glad Claud had been the first to make a move, to seek her out; it was almost as if they had quarrelled. Perhaps they had. She hoped he would come again. He is not too like his father, she thought as she washed the dishes. I shall go to those lectures on psychology. I may be too late to learn how to cope with a manic-depressive husband, but I can learn to understand Claud.

Claud, on his way home, felt pleased with himself. He had done the right thing visiting his mother. She was okay. Would it be possible to meld parts of his mother into the small character based on Ann Kennedy? Why not, good idea. An old man standing by a tree in the lane apparently having a leak waved. Claud waved back as he swung round a corner. The whisky bottle toppled but he caught it before it fell. Had she noticed that he had stolen her sleeping pills? He patted his pocket with the bottle of pills in it. She is happy now, she doesn't need these things. I shall keep them just in case I get so worried by my work I lose sleep. I cannot afford to lose sleep. The only loss I will put up with is through Laura.

Helen Peel reminded her husband that ages ago she had given him an errand for Laura. Had he been yet? It was weeks since—

'No, not yet', 'Sorry, I forgot', 'I'll do it next week', 'Thanks for reminding me, I'll make a note—'

'We are into February, I want that god in place by April when the garden is open in aid of the blind – it has a missing hand.'

'The blind wouldn't notice anything missing—'

'What a heartless thing to say! What a crude sort of joke.'

'It was not a joke, a mere remark.'

'I believe your mother was right to call you pedantic.' (Helen always referred to her mother-in-law as though she were dead.)

'What's my mother got to do with—'

'Nothing, thank the Lord, but please, Christopher, I am serious. Get that job done for me, I don't want to have to—'

(Deal with Laura yourself.) 'Okay,' said Christopher. 'I'll tie a knot in my hanky, make a note, get cracking. Don't worry, old girl, it shall be done.'

Why should I run her bloody errand? Christopher asked himself. Because she doesn't like Laura, she's afraid of Laura, afraid of Laura's tongue. Laura had made a *sotto voce* joke when Helen had the garden open last year in aid of the spastics. It had sent John and Emma into a gale of giggles. He had not heard the joke himself, nor asked to have it repeated. They had told their grandmother and Rose had gasped with pleasure. 'What superlative bad taste!' Rose would never laugh at spastics so one guessed the joke was to do with Helen, quite possibly himself. One seldom saw Rose these days, married to that fellow, but she'd always got on well with Laura, there was something deeper than the usual female alliance between those two.

John and Emma in their teens were tiresome enough; what would they be like if they were Laura's children? An alarming idea. Much better to be safe with Helen, one knew where one was with Helen. She would not let John and Emma fall under Laura's influence, or his mother's, for that matter; she knew how to protect her family. Christopher felt warm affection for his wife. Her head was screwed on the right way.

Okay, he thought, I'll see she gets the statue's hand fixed. It isn't often she entrusts me with anything to do with the garden. As for John and Emma, there was no proof, but he was sure it was one or other or both who had vandalised the statue. It had been all in one piece when Helen bought it. Christopher chuckled. He did not suppose either of his offspring had intended doing their father a good turn when they chopped the hand off. He looked forward to visiting Laura, was glad to have a valid excuse.

Christopher hummed on his way to the station the following day. A little delay, a spot of pleasurable anticipation, no mad obvious rush to see Laura and perhaps Helen would stop nagging and harping about one's old loves? There was comfortable time to call in on Laura before the directors' meeting. One could catch up with her news. (Had one ever even lagged behind with her news, she was such a bloody clam? Ha, ha, quite a good joke, one could use it again some time.) Make a discreet enquiry or two to find out whether there was still anything up with that Wog composer from behind the Iron Curtain. Imagine fancying a Communist, it boggled one's imagination. A Red! God! Really! It must be vicious gossip – really what some people's minds – and what about that boy? One had seen her with him. One could find out about him, discreetly, of course. Did he have anything to recommend him? Youth? Christopher stopped humming. Bloody youth. That polished buttercup hair. The features not yet moulded by experience. Where had he read that? In one of Helen's library books? Some soppy woman writer, never read a woman writer, they so often had a pinko tinge.

Christopher caught his train, and all the way to London pictured Laura as she had been and how she might have been had she not – had she not chosen to go her own way. She never had any intention of marrying me, he thought with painful clarity as the train passed Maidenhead. Those few times they had fumbled and tumbled and rolled about in his bed during the Easter holidays when the parents were out had been what she had quite frankly said at the time purely experimental. God! thought Christopher in his middle age, she was a bloody little cock-teaser in those days. It may have been experimental for her, he thought, but for me, he thought, blanching at the memory, well, really, even now after all these years I burn. (Well, simmer.)

Gathering up his *Times* and *Spectator*, putting *Private Eye* into his briefcase – one couldn't really be seen carrying it – Christopher damped his recollections of the unassuaged lusts of adolescence, squared his shoulders, checked his fly, and stepped off the train at Paddington Station. Here he walked fast to the cab rank and, stepping determinedly ahead of a flustered old woman with a heavy suitcase, settled himself into a taxi.

'Where to?' asked the driver.

Christopher gave Laura's business address. The driver turned up the volume of his radio. He was listening to the Test match.

One wondered why one saw Laura so rarely, Christopher thought as the taxi shot past Sussex Gardens. One needn't wonder, he thought sourly as it jerked to a stop at the lights. Helen would not countenance one's seeing much more of Laura than one did. As the taxi whizzed along the Bayswater Road and dodged nippily into the park one agreed that the other reason one saw so little of Laura was Laura's marked lack of enthusiasm. I shan't tip this man, he drives far too fast, how can he pay attention to what he's doing when his mind is on those jokers down under?

One had arrived.

Christopher fumbled for change. God, these pound coins did one's pockets damage, it was a wonder they didn't shoot down one's leg into one's shoe. 'What's the score?'

The driver took the money, did not answer; he was black, Jamaican probably. He turned the radio higher, grinned suddenly at Christopher, shouted, 'We's winning, brother!' and drove off.

Christopher made careful way down area steps and walked along a covered passage to the door which had 'Laura Thornby, Repairs and Restoration, please ring' on it. Here, in the basement of an anonymous building, Laura plied her trade.

Standing at the door Christopher wondered why this was the only address he had for Laura apart from the Old Rectory, which she seldom visited. Where did she live in London? Not here. This was work, a place of business; there was not even a comfortable chair; did she perhaps live with someone, a man? A lover? Why had this possibility not struck him before? And if she did live with some bloke, how could one find out? People gossiped at home, but here in London nobody noticed what was going on; she vanished into London as into some black hole in space. Christopher put his thumb on the buzzer.

'Who is it?' Laura's voice, tinny and disembodied, whispered through the grille.

'Christopher.'

'Christopher who?'

'Christopher Peel.'

'Oh! Christopher Peel. One should have guessed. One should have known. Come in, how can one help you?' She opened the door. 'Step inside,' she said. He had interrupted her at work. He knew better than to rise to her teasing; if he was not careful she would keep it up for hours. One had wept as a child, been reduced to hitting her, pulling her hair out by the roots.

'I am on an errand for Helen,' he said. 'She has a statue she bought last autumn – it needs a hand.'

'It needs a hand. Does one have specifications?'

'Please, Laura.'

Laura said, 'You'd better come in.' She turned and led the way, he followed. 'But you can't stay long,' she said over her shoulder, 'I'm busy.'

Christopher tried to remember an occasion when she had not said this.

'All right.' She was wiping clay off her hands with a damp cloth. 'Let me write it down. Have you got the measurements?'

No messing about, no chit-chat, straight to business. 'Yes, actually I made a tracing of the stump, it's a clean break.' Christopher fished his wallet from the breast pocket of his pinstriped suit and extracted a piece of tracing paper. 'And a photograph of the original.'

'Very neat,' said Laura, taking them. 'Why don't you sit down?'

'I'd rather stand. I have to go on to a directors' meeting. I don't want to sit in some clayey mess.'

'Idiot.' Laura took a duster from her desk drawer and flipped it across the seat of a chair. 'There, sit on that, it makes me nervous having you standing over me. Or sit on this newspaper.' She spread a sheet of newsprint across the chair seat. 'The *Financial Times* should suit you.'

Christopher eyed the newspaper suspiciously. 'Another client left it here, it's not my kind of paper.' She laid the tracing on her desk and studied it.

Christopher sat uneasily, his hat on his knee. He

had never worn a hat until lately, but people seemed to be wearing them again and Helen said he looked right in this soft trilby. Ah, Helen. He looked disparagingly at the hat, hoped Laura would not comment. His eyes ranged round Laura's workroom. Nothing had changed since his last visit: the kiln stood against one wall, tubs of clay covered with wet cloths ranged opposite. There was her desk, the chair he sat on, the chair she sat on; shelves from floor to ceiling held tools and casts. Casts of hands, feet, parts of arms, legs, all ranged in sizes, a variety of heads and bowls which held examples of smaller portions of anatomy, fingers, toes, ears, noses and he supposed penises, though he had never actually seen one.

'I may have one that fits,' said Laura. 'It would save you a bob or two to have one ready made.'

Christopher took this as an aspersion or sideways dig at his frugal spending habits. He disliked the smell of Laura's workshop; the clay dust in the air made him sneeze. Looking about him, he caught the eye of Laura's cat crouching near the warm kiln. The cat was an extremely small pale grey tabby which matched the background. It stared at Christopher. Christopher looked away, discomfited by its amber eyes. The cat yawned, exposing a pale pink palate and useful teeth.

Laura was frowning and leafing through a ledger. Christopher wondered whether the dust in the air made her wash her hair every night; he would have liked to know this small intimacy. Did she shampoo it or only stand under the shower and rinse it through? She looked distant and preoccupied, businesslike in grey denim jeans, a grey sweatshirt. Lit by a harsh overhead light she melted, as did the cat, into the general greyness of the room. He said, 'You look so different when you are working.'

'And you presumably do not wear that pretty pinstripe when you are on the beach or in the garden.' She did not look up as she concentrated on her search. 'Ah, this should do you. Number sixty, exactly the right size. Casts I made from Nicholas when I was starting this business. He has beautiful hands.'

'Helen does not like Nicholas.'

'Helen would not know.'

'She might, she's extremely observant.'

'All right, since she's so particular, what about these, number seventeen. These?' She slewed the ledger round so that Christopher could see the photograph.

'But those are my hands. I remember.'

'Yes.' They both remembered an afternoon in the far past. She had laughed as she made casts of his hands one afternoon in the studio she had had in the Old Rectory.

'She'd know—' He was tempted but cautious.

'Rubbish. You were a lot younger.'

'She doesn't know, she has no idea I ever—'

'Oh, Christopher, be your age, Helen isn't as stupid as all that. It fits perfectly.'

'Well, I won't have it. It would be positively creepy.'

Laura said, 'Okay. Let's see what else—' She went on turning the pages. 'Mind you, I think Helen is silly to muck about with her statues, she should leave well alone. It's not of course in my interest to lose an order, but—'

'She can't stand mutilations—'

Laura stared across her desk daring Christopher to go on, knowing that given half a chance he would accuse her of mutilating him.

He had once actually done so, he had a habit of repeating himself. Christopher dropped his gaze. 'She was traumatised in the British Museum as a child.' He cleared his throat (all this dust).

Laura snorted. 'So she says! Personally I think she is wrecking the garden; it was perfect in your mother's day. It's not meant to be formal and Italianate, dotted about with fake Apollos.'

'Helen loathes disorder.'

'Your mother achieved a charmed dishevelment in that garden with those loopy clematis and vines, scrambling roses, unexpected lilies. Helen is ruining it. I hear she has dug up the iris beds.'

'It's not my mother's garden any more,' said Christopher stiffly. 'It's Helen's.'

'How right you are. Well, who am I to criticise your wife, my client?'

Christopher was silent. He wondered what would have happened to the garden if he had married Laura – he did not like Laura's tone – always supposing Laura had been agreeable.

Laura, for her part, suppressed a smile as she congratulated herself on having evaded this fate. 'I prefer you as a client,' she said.

'What?' (She had always known what he was thinking.)

'Here we are. Just the job. A recent model. Nice, aren't they?' (Time he made up his mind; this visit has gone on long enough.)

Christopher peered. 'Whose hands are they?'

'Nobody you know.'

'I hear you are interested in that Roumanian composer.'

'I've heard that too; conductor.'

'Are you?'

'These are not his hands. The interest was minimal.' Laura's patient voice held underlying threat.

Christopher said: 'People do gossip, you know.'

'I know. Will these do? I haven't got all day, Christopher, and there's your directors' meeting or whatever.'

'They look all right.' He was grudging. 'Sure they are not some criminal?'

'Christopher, your mind! I am not Madame Tussaud.'

'I like to know what I am living with. Every time I pass that statue I—'

Laura was laughing. 'It's not going to come to life and give you a mason's handshake. These hands have perfectly respectable provenance, I promise you.'

'Sure?'

'Sure.'

'Very well.' Christopher got to his feet. 'How soon can Helen have it?'

'I'll let you know. I'll post it and send instructions on how to—'

'I hoped you would do it for us.'

'You can manage—'

Still Christopher lingered. 'I - er - hear—'

'Yes?'

'Well, Helen, no, to be honest it was me. I saw you in the wine bar with some new friend.'

'Claud Bannister.'

'So *that's* who it was. Oh. Isn't he supposed to be writing a book? His mother told—'

'I believe he is.'

'So you are coming down oftener?'

'Who says?'

'I thought you must be interested when I saw you with him.'

'You did?'

'So naturally I thought when you next come down

you could fix the hand for Helen. I mean, when I heard, I mean saw, I—'

'What a lot you hear and see.'

'What?'

'What?'

'What I am getting at,' said Christopher, goaded, 'is, are you in love with him? Is he in love with you?'

'He is in love, poor fellow.'

Christopher said, 'You have lost none of your charm, Laura.'

'He's not in love with me, you fool.' Laura was irritated.

'Oh, oh, wrong end of the stick as usual. Who is he in love with, then, if it's not you?' Christopher found himself relieved, delighted even.

'Whoever it is may do him harm.'

'Would that matter?' (Would she mind?)

Laura did not answer; she watched Christopher thoughtfully.

'I don't believe I've met him since he grew up.' Christopher had never been averse to a spot of delving. 'I know his mother, of course, just to say hullo. She was a wartime evacuee who was almost not claimed by her parents; one is left wondering what sort of people they were. She married Bannister who drank and left her. One used to see him in the boozer. You must remember him.'

'Vaguely.'

'They weren't the sort of people we were likely to know, were they?'

'Who?' Laura's eyebrows rose at Christopher's patronising tone.

'The Bannisters, your protégé's parents.'

'I'd scarcely call him a protégé.' Laura side-stepped Claud.

'Well, whatever he is.' Christopher hesitated to proceed.

Making no effort to rescue him from his predicament, Laura waited with her head slightly tilted, her eyes fixed on his face, just not meeting his gaze, a perverse trick he remembered from childhood. He is getting to look awfully like his aged pa, she thought, and smiled, remembering how her mother Emily had teased and manipulated and manoeuvred Ned Peel. 'You are getting to look very like your father,' she said. 'We knew him all right. There's nothing of your mother in you, is there?'

'That's what Helen says, she's thankful.'

'Helen would be.' Laura's tone was dangerously neutral. 'Well now,' she said, 'it's time you went to your meeting, is it not? You've carried out Helen's little commission, found out that there is nothing between me and the red composer, and nothing between me and Claud Bannister – as though it were any business of yours – so, having ordered a hand for Helen's fake – it'll be a special order, I can't let her have it at cost price – you'd better trot.'

'Don't be like that. I'm not prying—'

'What else would you call it?' He's as bad as Nicholas, she thought, forever poking his nose into my life. Has he nothing to keep him occupied?

The small cat, seized by a crisis of digestion, darted now between Christopher's legs on its way to its litter box where, turning its back and lifting its tail, it assuaged its need. Christopher watched the cat's tail shiver, picked up his briefcase and hat, and backed away. 'Whew! Whiffy! Phew!'

'It's momentary. She covers it up.' Laura was amused by Christopher's repugnance. 'The last time I came to see you and Helen I trod in your enormous dog's turd in my best shoes—'

Mulling thoughts of Claud Bannister, Christopher moved towards the door. 'No doubt Nicholas will review this *oeuvre* when it is published,' he said, half surprised to find himself aligned with Nicholas.

'No doubt he will,' Laura answered lightly, too lightly, Christopher observed.

At the door he bent to kiss Laura's cheek, which smelt of clay dust. 'Goodbye,' he said.

'Goodbye.' Laura closed the door.

As he walked away he heard her tinny voice through the grille. 'I like your fancy hat.'

Standing on the pavement waiting for a taxi, Christopher felt rage. By hardly saying a word Laura had made him feel a snob for his remarks about the Bannisters, and a fool for prying into her private life; she had not even asked after John and Emma, or shown a gram of gratitude at being given Helen's commission. 'Oh, fuck the woman,' he cried as a taxi drew alongside in answer to his waving arm. 'To the City,' he shouted, unnecessarily loudly.

Laura sat in the chair vacated by Christopher. He was clever to threaten me with Nicholas. 'I never thought Christopher could be consciously dangerous,' she said to the cat. 'What power weak people possess.'

She jotted notes for Helen's order while part of her mind reviewed Christopher's character. Obstinate, patronising, a cultivated reputation for kindness. Perhaps she was wrong to think him weak? I should have let him think he was doing me a good turn in giving me this order for Helen's beastly statue. I should have made him feel good, resisted picking on Helen. I hate her for wrecking that lovely garden. 'Oh,' said Laura to the cat, who had resumed its position by the kiln, 'why do I feel protective? There is no need.' She had not imagined the malice in Christopher's suggestion that Nicholas might review Claud's book. The thought converged with a second idea, the idea that Claud in love might become vulnerable to excess. 'I don't see why I should feel responsible,' she said to the cat, 'it cuts across the grain of my nature.' The cat purred sleepily, a self-contained animal.

Laura tidied her workshop, put the ledgers back in place, washed her hands at a corner sink, picked up the cat and put it in a wicker cat basket, pulled on a heavy tweed coat. She extinguished the lights and went out, double-locking the door. With the cat on her knee, she travelled by bus to the corner of the street in Chelsea where she lived in an anonymous block of flats. Taking the lift to the top floor she was reminded of Claud by the maker's name. (May his spirit keep up.) She walked along a corridor similar to all the other corridors in the building and let herself into her flat. The flat consisted of two rooms, bedroom and sitting-room, a kitchenette and bathroom. A cat-flap led onto a small terrace; from the terrace the cat occasionally leapt onto the roof. Looking up from the street she had once seen its tiny figure perched high above the street, viewing the world. It was not the sort of cat to catch sparrows or pigeon; it seemed content with its inhibited life, made few demands. She let the cat out of its basket, opened a tin of catfood and fed it. Waiting for it to finish its meal, she picked up the empty saucer, washed it and put it away.

The flat was spick and span, every surface gleaming and dust-free; she had the minimum of furniture and what there was was of fine quality. The bookshelves on either side of the fireplace held books in prime condition. The mirror over the fireplace reflected the only picture in the room, a Boudin of a beach scene near Boulogne. She stripped off her work clothes and put them out of sight. She ran a bath and soaked for a long time, soaping the clay from her nails before shampooing her hair and rinsing it under the shower. She dressed in black velvet slacks and a black cashmere jersey, padding about the room barefoot. She had strong slender feet with unpainted toenails. When she had mixed herself a drink she would check the Ansaphone for messages, cook herself a bowl of pasta, read a book for an hour or two before going to bed. There she would lie listening to the traffic passing far below in the frosty street. At some time in the night the cat would join her in the bed, for she always woke to find it curled on the pillow. While she slept her turbulent thoughts would swirl and wrestle in her unquiet mind.

Christopher's visit had reminded her of his single visit to the loft in their adolescence, a visit which had taught her the value of privacy. It had taken days to rid the loft of his presence; the idea of his smell in the bed had lingered long after the reality was gone. She remembered shaking the bedclothes out of the window, frightening the nesting seagulls as she flapped them violently in the cool air.

About that time she resolved to have a flat of her own where nobody came other than herself.

In the Old Rectory, even after moving to the back of the house, blockading herself away from the front, she had not been free of her family; just as in the loft she was unable to prevent the occasional intrusion of the Kennedys. Now when she woke there would be nothing in the flat to impinge on her privacy. No book replaced out of line on the shelf, no wrinkle in a rug disturbed by an alien foot, nothing touched by hands other than her own, no lingering scent to revive memory, no trace of another being. She occupied her small flat as closely as a mollusc its shell, did not even share its space with a cleaning woman. All trace of occupation was absolutely hers.

Her lovers had had to put up with meetings in hotels; if they had flats of their own she would visit them there. This way she spared herself the risk of finding a nostalgic trace of a body, loved however briefly, in her bed.

She had not seen Claud for weeks, had stopped driving down the motorway at night to appear unannounced in his arms. It had become too pleasurable. 'If I threw away the key of the house I could spare myself this travail—'

Just before she fell asleep she noted a change in the sounds from the street: the frost had given way to rain.

Having climbed the ladder and lowered the trap-door Claud felt secure in the loft. Ann Kennedy's breakfasts were substantial, so for a while his blood cherished rather his digestive system than his brain. He dreamed as he listened to the seagulls circling the roofs as they might Beachy Head, swirling and screaming. Come spring, they would rest against the chimneys, and by the time their eggs hatched his manuscript would have matured into a novel, an exhilarating but daunting prospect.

During this digestive period, staring at the view of the river and the gasworks, Claud saw no view. He saw Laura, Mavis and Amy melded mysteriously into the girl with whom he was increasingly obsessed, who would, digestive process over, guide his fingers at the typewriter. She was so real that at times she ceased to be purely cerebral and he threw himself onto the divan and masturbated as he had in the throes of adolescence, falling then asleep to wake bemused and baffled by the force of his creation, whom he must now try to distil onto paper, so curbing self-indulgence.

He was, too, a little afraid of this enchanting creature, and some days, feeling he must distance himself from her, he turned his mind towards his market stall, busied himself sorting, pricing and packing his stock, forcing himself to stop dreaming so that he could make the money, as Laura had so practically suggested, to pay for the dreaming or, he would correct himself, for the writing, his real work.

She was still there, of course, on market days, his girl; she was not to be conveniently left in the loft. He was aware of her as he listened to the chatter of passers-by, watched Susie and Brian at the next stall, Brian joking and Susie shivering and tipping the scales with her pink mittened fingers, her lovely skin glowing in the winter air. He had, he felt, first-hand knowledge of Susie's skin for, just as his girl had Mavis' hair, she had Susie's skin and Laura's legs. The combination was effortlessly superior to any girl in the market. He hardly noticed, as the weeks passed and in every way his girl became more real, that she grew less and less like Amy, but frequently he worried that as yet she had no name. For he could not bring himself to name her. He knew this was stupid, infantile, superstitious even, but giving her a name would be to let her go, to abandon her to the world of readers.

(Curiously, it never occurred to Claud, otherwise so diffident, to question whether his book would find a publisher.)

So for his readers' use he hit on an acronym, and where all through the manuscript he had left a gap where his girl's name should be, he typed in May. (To make use of Amy back to front was all that she deserved.) He hoped that he would see her passing through the market and looked forward to shouting out, 'Hullo, May.' An unlikely event, since she lived at least a hundred miles away, but the use of the name May comforted him. If in the course of the book something hurtful and degrading should have to happen to his precious girl, he could imagine it happening to Amy, turned back to front, getting a merited comeuppance while his real girl went unscathed. Having solved this little problem Claud wrote much better than before and gave May a really brutal pasting, which improved the story and made him feel good.

Feeling good, he stopped looking on market day as a bind and began to enjoy it and take a pride in his stall. He took days off from his book and visited other towns, travelling by bus to buy oddities in charity shops or pick through dusty boxes of junk in dealers' back rooms, interesting men who visited the market and sometimes bought from him, giving him good prices for things his mother had given him and even better prices for Laura's original contributions. He was meticulous in the putting aside of Laura's share and looked forward to the time when her part of the stock would be sold and his stall be all his own.

This wishing to be rid of Laura's stuff was in part due to Nicholas and Emily Thornby's visits to the stall. They would linger, picking and fingering, speaking to each other in voices so like Laura's that his scalp crawled, as they hinted in audible asides that this thimble or that silver frame might be or was truly from their attic, implying by a jerk of an elbow or a toss of a pointed nose some possible dishonesty on someone's part, not necessarily Claud's. Claud knew their behaviour to be a tease intended to discomfort. They chuckled and glanced up at him with sliding eyes, always seeming on a lower level though they were both tall, and he, meeting Laura's eyes in their wrinkled faces, felt endangered. Had not Laura lain in his arms, wrapping her legs so cheerfully round him, and had he not purloined those legs for his girl?

There was something so excellent and carefree about Laura's legs and the use she made of them while love-making that he resented these same legs (which were, do not forget, his girl's legs, with whom he was obsessed) having any connection with the elder Thornbys standing there teasing him. Then, while he listened to them, pretending of course that he was busy with another customer, Claud would feel a mad longing for a refresher course of Laura, for it was many weeks since he had waked to find her in his bed wearing nothing but her jersey, and he would feel a fierce lust for Laura which had little to do with his girl, his lover, his obsession. To still these rather strange sensations Claud, one market morning as Nicholas and Emily fiddled with the objects on his stall, began to rearrange it, putting all that was left from the Old Rectory attic on one side. 'I'll make things easier for you,' he said. 'All this came from your daughter Laura, the rest I have collected or been given by my mother.'

The old people straightened their backs and stared at Claud. 'You are depriving two poor old people of a source of innocent entertainment,' said Emily crossly.

'And how is your book progressing?' asked Nicholas, all interest in the stall forgotten.

Claud flushed. 'My book?' Had Laura—?

'That pretty girl Mavis, the little actress, told her mother, who told the butcher, who told the baker, who told the milkman, who told us. What is your book about?' Nicholas wheedled.

'Machines,' said Claud quickly.

'Machines?' Emily expressed surprise. 'What sort?'

'Machines,' said Nicholas. 'Oh,' he said. 'Ah.'

'No lovely girls?' asked Emily.

'Or fascinating men?' enquired Nicholas.

Claud smiled insincerely, nervously.

'We supposed we had a writer among us with brilliant descriptive powers—'

'Lots of sex,' said Emily. 'One can't have enough.'

'Oh yes one can, Em. Don't listen to her, dear boy.'

Claud stepped back, fearing the imposition of intimacy as Nicholas persisted. 'Descriptive powers are what matters and what a head start you have lodging with Mrs Kennedy, low slung like a dachshund, with an arse like a Clydesdale mare. That's good, isn't it? Have you noticed her legs?'

'Not particularly,' said Claud, recognising the description as exact (poor Ann!).

'Oh, the pity! You must! Truncated legs the woman has, then she produced this almost legless woman, a delicious beauty like Mavis. Is not nature amazing?' Nicholas crowed.

'Or God,' said Emily. 'Give God credit.'

'My sister does not believe in God, but she likes to drag him in to the conversation to give tone,' said Nicholas.

'Or Her, don't you think God's female, Mister—' pursued Emily, 'Bannister.' (She knew his name all right.) 'Claud.'

'It,' said Nicholas. 'Definitely It. But to revert to the Kennedys' legs—'

'If you came to visit us instead of Laura - didn't you come to read the meter once? - we could discuss your opus.' Emily changed tack.

'His *oeuvre*,' said Nicholas. 'We review, you know, or perhaps you don't.'

'I expect he has the sense to keep quiet until it's finished,' said Emily. 'Come on, Nicholas, we really must stop dawdling.'

'What was all that in aid of?' asked Brian from the next stall.

'I've no idea,' said Claud, but he felt threatened and decided to pack up early and get back to his typewriter and his girl. Laura's relations had put Laura out of his head, but as he let himself into the Kennedy house he thought of her again.

Ann Kennedy shouted from the kitchen, 'You're back early. Like some lunch?'

'No thanks,' answered Claud.

'There's plenty for two. I used to give Laura a snack if I heard her come in.'

Claud paused, one foot on the stair. 'What did she do in the loft, Ann?'

'Laura? Nothing.'

'Nothing?'

'Nothing.'

'Oh—'

'Well, like you, she was pretty private. Always very quiet, just like you, no visitors, no lovers, nothing. Nothing for all those years.'

'Oh.' (What a lot Ann Kennedy failed to hear.)

'I was glad, of course, that she kept the key; it was nice to feel she had a refuge.'

'Oh.'

'Even if she didn't use it.'

'Yes.' Claud waited, but Ann said no more. 'Well, I must do some work,' he said.

Does she know how often Laura has been here to visit me? he wondered as he climbed the stair. Too late to ask her not to gossip. What does it matter? He pushed up the trap-door. Here I am, he thought.

His typewriter sat where he had left it, the pile of manuscript grown quite substantial, but there was no girl.

The sun shone in splashing the floor with light, the seagulls screamed, but his mind was empty. In rushed despair. He could not remember Susie's skin, he could not remember Amy, Mavis' hair could be any hair on any girl's head, he could not remember Laura's legs, everything was suddenly black and devoid of meaning. What on earth possessed me to think I could write? My confidence is pseudo, he thought. He remembered telling Laura that he would kill himself if he failed. Had he been serious? How then to set about it?

He sat at the typewriter and typed:

Hanging. If I bought a rope, I could swing a rope over one of the beams, stand on a chair and kick off. What did Mavis do with the webbing we used to haul up the stove? The undertaker connection would strike a suitably macabre note. But oh, the gagging purple face, the bulging eyes. I'd prefer to look decent in death.

Claud stood up and examined his face in a small mirror propped on the bookshelf.

Cut my wrists? he typed. I have a razor. But think of

the mess. Poor Ann. I could wrap myself in sheets and towels to prevent drips through the ceiling. Have I the nerve?

Overdose? Mother's pills are not lethal, I remember she said so to Pa when he was threatening suicide. She had said they might only make him sick. She hadn't believed him. Really, one's parents! Could I get my own pills? More pills? How many? But don't they pump you out? What indignity. One could, of course, put one's head in a plastic bag to make sure. But that was unnecessarily scary.

Drowning. I hate cold water. Fool, it would be a faster death. Perhaps I should give it priority. Cold kills quickly.

Jump off a cliff. What cliff? Where? We are miles from the sea. Would the church tower do? Could I get up it? Is it locked? Would it be sacrilege? Does God exist? What would I think as I fell through the air? And once again it's messy, nasty.

Throw myself under a train? What about the driver's feelings? (Find out about automatic trains.)

Electrocution. Is there a fire in the house with a long enough flex to reach the bath? Terribly painful. No dignity.

Laughing? People do not die laughing.

Heart attack? It took Father years of drinking to pull his off. Can't spare the time.

Shoot myself? No gun. No nerve. Too noisy.

Hunger strike? You must be joking.

Grief? Despair? Broken heart?

What an *embarras du choix.*

When he had finished the list Claud went over to the bed and lay down, rolled in the foetal position. He was too overwhelmed by despair to search for the cause. He had assumed in his besotted state that all was well, his writing a work of genius. There had been no self-doubts, not lately, anyway.

Lying in his hedgehog position he supposed his confidence gone for ever and began to repeat to himself ways and means of committing suicide.

The trouble, he thought, stretching his legs and turning onto his back, was that each method carried with it an element of failure. He would be too scared to pull it off, he had not thought it through, he would make a laughing stock of himself. Then he thought, That horrible old man was only teasing, why should I be afraid of him? His remark about being a book reviewer was more joky than malign. I must not be paranoid, he was trying to get a rise. What would Amy with the Walkman think of me lying shivering here?

For the first time for months he thought of Amy giggling and joggling in his protesting arms, turning the penetration of her parts into an obstacle course.

Claud began to laugh.

I should have hit her, he thought, bashed her about a bit. He sat up feeling purged.

I am shot of Amy, he thought. Then he thought, I am being too sentimental about May (he did not notice that he quite naturally called his girl May). What I need is more tension, a sharpening of focus if May is to pass muster with the reviewers and of course Laura—

He sprang off the bed, tore the typed list of deaths from the typewriter and pinned it to the wall. 'Come on, May,' he said out loud. 'Let's be having you.

'What we need,' he said, turning over the manuscript to chapter one, page one, 'is some tightening up, local colour, realistic descriptions of characters. So far I have concentrated on my darling. I shall use

Nicholas; describing him will be fun, a good exercise. And I must cut out a lot of blah.'

Claud sharpened a red pencil and whistled through his teeth. Outside the gulls had stopped shrieking and it had started to rain. He pulled the wastepaper basket closer to the desk.

All through the afternoon he used the red pencil with gusto.

He tore up whole sheets of typescript and stuffed them into the wastepaper basket. As he worked,despair dwindled to zero. When the winter light failed he switched on his lamp. He worked through the night, making merciless use of the red pencil, tearing and crushing bits of typescript, stamping them into the wastepaper basket with his foot.

At last, when the pubs had long closed and traffic in the town ceased to rumble and swish through the wet streets, and only the church clock dared break the silence, he stood up, stretched his arms above his head, eased his aching back. He felt groggy, exhausted, at peace.

The wastepaper basket was full, the unwieldy pile of typescript reduced to a skeleton, the red pencil blunted.

Swaying with fatigue, he sharpened the pencil. Never again would he ignore it. He stuffed the contents of the wastepaper basket into a plastic carrier bag which he put by the trap-door. He opened the attic window and, standing on a chair, peed into the night. He shut the window, shivering at the cold air, pulled off his clothes and crashed into bed. As he lay down he felt pleasantly intoxicated and thought of Laura, imagining her in his arms. He would pull off her jersey, hold her warmly. Did he not love her? Was she not responsible for the catharsis of the day? Had he in his awful fear and despair invoked her? He could not remember. He reproached himself that drivelling on about his fantasy girl all those weeks he had neglected Laura, pushing her into the background. There was more to Laura than legs.

Claud chortled sleepily, remembering Laura's legs with a sharp prick of desire and the simultaneous thought that Laura would be the last person to tolerate all that mush in the wastepaper basket about Amy/May. She may never know, he thought, but she is responsible for my whittling down of a whole heap of typescript into a work of some coherence. (In his state of sleepy euphoria it did not bother Claud that he was making Laura responsible for a work she had not read.) Thank God, Claud thought, that she refused to read it when I offered it to her. Then he thought paradoxically, I can still love May if I keep her in the proper context. Lastly, he thought before falling into an exhausted sleep, I shall take that bag of rubbish to Laura as an offering.

In her bed in the anonymous block of flats Laura lay wakeful and uneasy. Christopher's visit had revived a host of irritations usually suppressed, reminding her of a past she had put behind her. She did not want to feel sorry for him or made to feel guilty. Useless to think that if she had married Christopher she would have saved him from becoming a bore; it was not marriage to Helen which had precipitated his state, he was inclined that way from birth, taking after his father. She had wasted much breath trying to persuade him that the warmth and affection she felt for him risked turning to hate if knit by marriage. He had refused to accept and she in self-defence had grown mocking and distant.

But she could not forget Christopher's father's long and complex relationship with Emily. She had loved him for his goodness, his devotion to Emily, an extraordinary feat – almost guileless – of keeping faith not only with Emily but with his wife. Had he suffered guilt as he paid her school bills? He had, she suspected, rather enjoyed his situation, thought of himself as a bit of a dog. His wife Rose kept him on a tight rein while Emily, who was never a bore, amused and shocked. If only Helen had been ready to learn from her mother-in-law's example, or taken a leaf from Emily, her life would be merrier, her two children less lumpen. No responsibility of mine, thought Laura, turning on her side, away from the real intruding responsibility, the unwelcome load she could not shed. For if Ned Peel was not her father then most probably, and facing it honestly, as she had taught herself, Nicholas was both father and uncle. And it had not been so much to escape marriage with Christopher years ago that had precipitated flight, but home itself, those two, Emily and Nicholas, who had stuck in her young judgmental gullet.

She had denied them love.

And now, Laura thought as the small grey cat joined her in the bed, climbing up by her feet, its claws making tiny clicking sounds as it proceeded along the billowing duvet coming to rest on the pillow, Emily has grown old, Nicholas is old too, and my conscience nags and drags because I love them.

'I am responsible for you.' She tickled the cat's jaw. 'It's easy to love you. I don't mind that.' The cat purred, she felt the vibration along her finger. 'I lie here counting my responsibilities, listening to the rain. I wish, I wish I could sleep.' Outside the slanting rain splashed on the balcony, dripped from the eaves, gurgled down the drainpipe. I would like Christopher better if I could be friends with Helen, she thought. There must be something about Helen I could like. Could I, for instance, get her to admit that she likes her dog better than her children, which I am sure is the case? That would be a start. But she is such a conventional woman. She has no trace of Nicholas and Emily's charm, their total lack of humbug.

'What am I grumbling about?' she said out loud to the cat. 'I have fewer responsibilities than most, no husband, no children. I have kept away from Claud. If I work at it I shall soon reduce my feelings for him to a proper level. It's about time I gave him up entirely. He has lasted too long, does not fit my short-term norm,' she exclaimed aloud, annoying the cat who snuggled closer into the pillow as Laura, restless, got out of bed and padded to the window to stare out at the rain.

She switched on the Ansaphone to check whether any message needed immediate action.

A new message had been recorded in the last hour, a message from Nicholas: 'Emily and I have the flu. We are very ill. Mrs Datchett will not look after us as she says her husband comes first, which is rich since he died three days ago. Does the silly cow think she has the instant entrée into the underworld? One asks oneself would it be too much to invite you to tear yourself away from whoever's arms enwrap you to attend to your familial responsibilities? It is many weeks since you deigned to visit us.' Nicholas' voice trailed to a stop.

Laura replayed the message, trying to gauge whether Nicholas sounded ill; he was quite capable of indulging in a jape for the hell of it.

She stood for a while hesitating, then said to the cat, 'Come on, puss, responsibilities call.' The cat curled herself into a tighter ball.

She dressed and as she dressed admitted to herself that it was many weeks since she had been down to see them, that she had promised herself to tidy the Old Rectory garden last autumn. She had neglected it, and Emily and Nicholas, while enjoying herself with Clug. Clug who had fitted so perfectly into the principle of 'short term' that he scarcely left a wavemark. As she dressed, piling on warm clothes, arming herself against the winter night, she thought again of Claud, shocked by the warmth of her thoughts, telling herself that she should have snubbed him, nipped whatever was starting in the bud. She had let herself behave completely out of kilter, been reprehensibly light-hearted, no better than Nicholas, irresponsible, and here she was still eager to meet him, ambivalent, in danger of becoming besotted.

Her anxious mood infected the cat who swished her tail and scratched as Laura put her in the basket.

It might be best, she thought, not to tell Claud she had come back.

Carrying the cat, Laura let herself out of her flat into the deserted corridor and walked along to the lift. As she walked she regretted leaving her warm and orderly flat, her calm London existence. As the lift took her down to the basement garage her spirits, already low, sank lower. She put the cat basket on the seat of the car, drove up the ramp and headed west through the rain to the motorway. She switched on the car radio but quickly turned it off, nauseated by the *bonhomie* of an early disc-jockey, preferring the hiss of tyres on the wet road and the rhythmic clunk of the windscreen wiper. As her guilt feelings towards

Emily and Nicholas hounded her down the motorway, she thought enviously of ordinary, happy, uncomplex families at liberty to love each other. With the coming of daylight she dimmed the car's lights and took note of the passing country. She had last driven up in the death of winter. Now spring was making a start; there were occasional clumps of snowdrops and aconites on the verges, relics of gardens bulldozed to make room for the motorway, flights of mallard crossing the lightening sky from one reservoir to another. She drove away from the rain into brighter weather.

At the turn-off from the motorway she stopped to fill up with petrol, remove her drab jersey and put on instead a bright red one, topping it with a purple wool cap; if she wore clashing colours in the country, gossips would comment on her get-up rather than the expression on her face. She drove on, hoping that Nicholas and Emily's flu, if it existed, would not have engendered too mischievous a mood and might allow her a few days' peace in her quarters at the back of the house and some therapeutic work in the garden. 'I shall make a bonfire,' she said to the cat, 'and you shall go mousing.' She smiled, remembering Claud's surprised eye ranging round the disorderly room when he had come that first time, and that he had half-believed the caraway seeds in the cake were droppings.

Coming to a stop in the Old Rectory drive, she was careful not to slam the car doors. She let herself into her flat and released the cat. The room smelled cold, musty and damp; she crouched by the fire and struck a match, setting light to the tinder. After some initial hesitation the flames caught and roared up the chimney, sweeping with them the clammy air. Laura crouched, feeding the fire with twigs, then logs until the heat built up. The cat came close to roast its chest in the warmth.

She brought the duvet from her bedroom to air and switched on the electric water heater, listening with pleasure to the water gurgle in the pipes. She fed the cat and put fresh water out for it, set a kettle to boil for coffee.

Drinking her coffee, she watched the birds in the garden and planned her bonfire. She would cut back the buddleia and prune the forsythia neglected last autumn; she would trim the philadelphus and rake up the soggy leaves so that the air could get at the grass and the bulbs get a chance to shoot; she would collect the fallen branches from the apple trees; the bonfire would smell wonderful.

But first she must attend to Nicholas and Emily. She let the cat out into the garden, walked round the house and let herself in at the front door.

For a few moments she stood in the hall, listening. Her grandfather's long-case clock tocked in a corner; upstairs Nicholas coughed. As her eyes grew accustomed to the light, she saw the hall table littered with opened letters, a newspaper, a vase of dead flowers. Beyond it the umbrella stand, which she had forgotten until now, had held that shabby but distinguished umbrella belonging to the stranger who had helped her get drunken Nicholas and intoxicated Emily into the house and onto the drawing-room sofas and then Bonzo had ungratefully bitten him. No! It was Emily who had bitten him and when Bonzo had attacked he had said: 'Die for Eastbourne.' Where on earth did he spring from?

As Bonzo, having heard her, rose from his basket in the kitchen and came hurrying to greet her, Laura began to laugh. She greeted the dog and set off up the stairs in high good humour, resolving as she went to be agreeable to her parents, make light of her responsibilities, enjoy them.

Nicholas and Emily were sitting up in bed when Laura and Bonzo arrived upstairs.

'Darling!' exclaimed Emily. 'You came.'

'Answered our distress signal. What a trooper you are,' cried Nicholas.

Laura sat on the edge of the bed, smiling. 'Not dead yet, I see,' she said, 'nor do you seem to be dying.' She leaned forward to peruse their faces, rather flushed and blotchy. 'What a couple of old frauds!'

'We are seriously ill,' protested Nicholas. 'The doctor has given us antibiotics.'

'Good.'

'He listened to our chests with his thingy; said mine was like a squeezebox, terrible.'

'He said my nipples are like a baby's.' Emily laughed, her laughter choking into a wheeze.

'Don't laugh,' said Nicholas. 'It makes you worse. A new doctor, Laura, a personable young man, the very sight of him made Emily feel better. He might do for you.'

'Nobody will do for her,' said Emily.

'No.' Both old people choked with laughter.

Laura poured water and passed a glass to each patient. She wondered what the personable doctor had made of this pretty pair.

'Of course Nicholas was in his own room while the visit went on,' wheezed Emily, catching Laura's eye.

'Of course,' murmured Laura, surprising a strong rush of affection for the invalids. Look at it this way, she told herself, these two have been faithful for life, give or take a stumble or stray, a slight vagary. Their love may be a deviation from the norm, but it has lasted. They have known what they wanted and stuck to it. Why should they bother? If their mode of life has ruined mine, why should they care? There are many virtuous people who do more harm with their good intentions than this pair of hedonists.

She sat watching Nicholas and Emily lying propped by pillows in the double bed. Bonzo, crawling up over their feet, had settled between them lying on his back, eyes closed, mouth slightly open, tail gently wagging, adding his doggy smell to the fustiness of the sick-room, the tumbled bed and crumpled sheets.

'We wore our best nighties for the doctor's visit,' volunteered Emily. 'I wore the pink satin job given me long ago by dear old Ned.'

'Almost a museum piece. She topped it with her white lace shawl from Peru,' said Nicholas.

'Nicholas wore his navy silk pyjamas with the monogram across his tit.'

'I bet the doctor was impressed,' said Laura. 'I suggest,' she said, 'that you let me make up the bed with clean sheets while you have a bath—'

'Ooh. Dare we risk it?'

'Your nails are filthy and I bet the rest of you is the same. I'll scrub your backs. To be honest, you smell.'

'Listen to her!'

'And I'll fill your hot water bottles.'

'Just as Nanny did in the long gone nursery days!'

'It will not be the first time I have done it.' Laura ran the bath, filling the old-fashioned tub with a mahogany surround, a bath so large it easily held two people. 'Come on, in you get,' she said.

'The Nazis made people bath before they gassed them,' Emily whispered loudly to her brother.

'Careful, careful. Oops, it's hot.' Nicholas tested the water with his toe before lowering himself into the bath. 'Come on, ducks.' He held out his hand to his sister.

Laura took clean sheets from the airing cupboard and made up the bed, turning Bonzo off to do so. She also opened a window to let fresh air blow in. She chucked the dirty sheets out onto the landing, closed the window and turned her attention to the two in the bath. 'Let's be scrubbing you.'

'You're so bossy.' Nicholas dipped down into the hot water.

'I bet the doctor said you could have a bath.' Laura took Emily's hands and brushed her nails. 'How could you let them get like this?' She did not expect an answer.

'Actually, yes, he did say it could be risked. We rather took it to mean at some future date.'

'Hum.'

'One wonders whether this is not some ploy of yours to give us pneumonia, get rid of us.'

'I wouldn't do that, I love you.'

'Ho, ho! She loves us, listen to that,' exclaimed Emily. 'Love!'

'I think that's enough.' Laura straightened her back after sponging Nicholas. 'Let's wrap you in hot towels and put you into clean things.'

'It's supposed to be people with uneasy consciences who bother about soap. Oh, look at the colour of the water, Emily, that was all us.'

'Yuk,' said Emily. 'You dirty old man.'

Laura hustled them back into bed, tucked them in and plumped up their pillows. She took Bonzo downstairs and sent him out into the garden while she boiled a kettle for the hot bottles. Waiting for the water to boil, she wondered how Nicholas and Emily, particular about nice things and a presentable house, could endure so much physical dirt, being both able to lie for hours in a bath without ever using soap or nailbrush. They must have india-rubber consciences, she thought, and warded off feelings of anger and frustration, familiar and useless. Better, she thought, screwing the top onto a hot bottle, to love them as they are, stop judging. She called the dog and went back to her parents carrying the hot bottles.

Nicholas had brushed his sparse hair and put on clean pyjamas. Emily lay against the pillows pursing her mouth. 'We hope it's allowed, we changed our minds about my nightie and his pyjamas and put on others. It's all right, we put your choice back in the drawers.' She grinned like a child.

(They don't look like – like what? They look like ordinary old people – perhaps they are.) 'Should you take your pills now?' Laura asked (but they do look very frail now they are clean).

'About now, yes.' Nicholas nodded hard to show willing. 'Four times a day the doctor said.'

'What have you had to eat?'

'We haven't felt like eating.' Emily's pathetic accents would wring the best of withers.

'Okay. Lie back, relax, take your medicine, I'll take care of you.' Laura dished out pills, popping one into each obedient mouth. 'I'll do some shopping, get you some grapes. Has Mrs Datchett really lost her husband?'

'He's not lost. She buried him as Bonzo does his bones,' said Nicholas.

'I see that you are feeling better. I'll stay until you are quite well.'

'Oh, goody!' said Emily. 'Would it be too much to ask

you to bring up the television?'

'All right.'

'Most noble,' said Nicholas. 'What a saintly girl.'

'I am going to do some work in the garden when I've finished with you.'

'Most therapeutic.' Emily coughed.

'Any chance of a little nip?' enquired Nicholas.

'Nips don't mix with antibiotics.'

'Oh, God, what a life,' sighed Emily.

'Don't start complaining or she'll beat it to London and leave us to die, won't you, darling?'

'I - well - might,' agreed Laura. 'There's not much to keep me here.'

'What about—' Emily began.

'Watch it,' Nicholas hissed and slapped his sister's hand.

It is admirable in its way, the way they never let up, thought Laura, guessing that Emily was hinting at Claud.

'Some flowers would add nicely to the décor.' Nicholas looked appreciatively round the bedroom which Laura had been tidying as they talked.

'I'll see what the garden can provide. What's all this?' she asked, catching sight of an assortment of objects on a side-table.

'We bought them back.' Nicholas watched her reaction. 'We enjoy picking over his knick-knacks' stall. We think we should support the arts. He's writing a book, your toy boy, did you know?'

'Yes.' Laura tossed their dirty nightclothes out onto the landing, suppressing the impulse to hit one or both the old persons, noting that her rare rush of affection was draining rapidly.

'We shall be better tomorrow,' said Nicholas hoarsely.

'She's afraid we shall be,' said Emily, who read Laura's face better than her brother.

'Don't push your luck, I'm not strong enough,' said Nicholas.

Laura carried the sheets and pillowcases down and put them in the washing machine. She made soup and while it brewed she cut branches of forsythia buds from the garden and set a vase where they could see it from the bed. She brought up the television. As she worked, she tried to persuade herself that Nicholas had not actually threatened Claud. She must not become paranoid. What harm could he do?

Presently she went out in her car and did some necessary shopping. When she returned she fed the old people with soup and fruit and switched on the television. They were a little flushed by now, still coughing but beginning to get sleepy.

In the garden she raked leaves into piles, pruned and cut back shrubs, heaping the branches and twigs onto a high pile of leaves. Her spirits improved with the work. When the sheets were washed, she hung them on the line to be blanched by the moon, crisped by the frost. She was pleased by the company of the resident robin who discovered treats which she had exposed with her raking.

She filled the wheelbarrow with logs from the store, stacked up the log baskets in the house and brought a load to her own quarters. Her rooms were warm now and homely. Before lighting her bonfire she kicked off her rubber boots and went upstairs to look in on the invalids.

Children's hour was playing on the television; Nicholas and Emily were asleep. They looked old and rather ill, innocent, their mouths agape.

Tired but happy, she returned to the garden to light her bonfire. Crouching beside it, putting a match to dry leaves, she watched the flame hesitate then leap from leaf to leaf and the whole begin to glow as she fed it with twigs, then heavier sticks and branches. As the aromatic smoke swirled up she stacked and padded up the fire so that the whole heap of rubbish would combust and burn through the night, leaving only a ring of ash in the morning. At some time in the night, she promised herself, she would wake and come to the door and breathe in the nostalgic scent of past autumns and winters.

When Bonzo rushed barking at a man coming round the side of the house she automatically shouted: '*Die*—' and Bonzo stopped in his tracks, growling. She said, 'Who is it?'

The man said, 'Laura, it's me, Claud,' and Laura jumped into his arms.

'Oh Laura, Laura, how delicious you smell, woodsmoke and pepper. I saw your car in the town. I was venturing to bring you your share of the stall money and hoping you would be pleased. I brought you crumpets. Are you cross? Are you glad to see me? It is so long since—'

'Why should I be cross?'

'You looked so happy by your fire in the twilight. Have you noticed the sunset, the red sky? And your red trousers and bright jersey, so happy alone I feared to interrupt. Is he going to bite me?'

'No, no. Stop sniffing and growling, Bonzo, stop.'

'And I have to tell you the good news about my book.'

'Is it finished?'

'No, but it will be. I have pared it down to the bare jokes. Can I kiss you again?'

'Of course. Come in, tell me all your news. Listen, while I settle Emily and Nicholas for the night, will you care for my fire and toast the crumpets?'

'Are they ill?' (She did not notice my joke.)

'Flu, that's all. Then we can sit by the fire and have tea. What time is it?'

'About six. This dog makes me nervous; he looks hungrily at my legs.'

'His little way. I will take him up to Nick and Em. Come, Bonzo.' Bonzo followed Laura, grumbling. 'And when we've had tea,' she said over her shoulder, 'we can go to bed.'

'And I can read you my book.'

'And that, too,' said Laura. 'Or you could read it to me after, that would be even nicer.'

While Laura, tired from her exertions in the garden, changed her clothes, Claud made tea and toasted crumpets.

'I have brought you your share of money for the things you gave me for my stall,' he said. 'I was planning to give it to your mother, or ask her to give me your address in London so that I could send it you.'

Laura squatted on the hearthrug. 'I am stiff,' she said. 'Unused muscles ache.' She took the envelope of money. 'I see that Nicholas and Emily have contributed to your trade; they seem to have bought back a lot of things.' She opened the envelope, counted the money.

'Are they mad?' Claud buttered the crumpets.

'Not mad, naughty. What a lot of money!' Laura poured tea, drank. 'This is good, I need it. What an astute business man you have become,' she teased.

'I enjoy my stall apart from your relations'

visitations.' Claud had half-expected Laura to refuse the money, tell him to keep it since the stock it represented was back if not in the attic, at least in the Old Rectory; he was after all a struggling artist. But Laura gave no hint of doing so.

Guessing his thoughts, Laura decided that such a move would pander to his incipient weakness; she would give the money to Oxfam. She put the envelope on the mantelshelf. Looking at Claud in the light of the fire she thought he looked older, more vulnerable. His slightly blurred features had sharpened during her absence; he was more adult, his attractiveness increased. 'My mother does not know my address, only my phone number.'

'So secret? Not even your mother?'

'Particularly not my mother. She could, perhaps, if she'd be bothered, give you my address at work; it's in the telephone book.'

'Oh.' Claud felt foolish. 'Is where you live as private as the loft used to be?' he asked.

'Yes.'

'But you will tell me?' He was confident.

Others had been equally confident. Laura did not answer. She sat cross-legged eating crumpets, drinking tea. The firelight sent shadows dancing across her face, invented red lights in her hair. Fat chance, she thought. She said: 'I must settle my invalids for the night, then your novel shall have my undivided attention.' She kissed his cheek, stood up.

'I thought—'

'We could do that afterwards, surely the novel is the most important?' she said.

Claud thought it too difficult to explain that the novel was the loving and the loving was in large part Laura. He watched her go, then heaped the used tea things on a tray and put it by the sink, hesitating whether to wash up. He decided against; he might break a precious cup, chip the already chipped pot. 'No seed cake today,' he said out loud. He peered into the bedroom. Laura's gardening clothes lay in a heap, red trousers, yellow shirt, violet sweater. From the centre of the bed the small cat watched. 'You'll soon have to move,' Claud threatened the cat. The animal's yellow eyes gave nothing away. Claud said, 'Shoo.' The cat did not stir; he would have liked to throw something, to give it a fright, but he went back to the hearth, stacked more wood on the fire, waited for Laura.

There was really very little of the novel left to read. He could, though, tell her the tale; it was clear in his head. He could read her the few extracts that were left, the excellent description of her legs, the paragraph about Mavis' hair, the description of Susie's skin. I wish she would hurry back, he thought. 'I thought you were never coming,' he said as she came through the door.

'I am here now,' she said, looking down at him. 'Shall you start reading?'

Claud reached up to her waist, hooking his fingers in her waistband. 'There is hardly anything left of the book to read,' he said, undoing the button of her jeans. 'But I can quote you the best passage, which is about your legs.' He unzipped her fly. 'I destroyed so much but it is all there, in my head, ready to flow onto the typewriter.' Kneeling, he drew the jeans down from her waist. 'Your dream legs keep me awake at night in a state of frustrated lust. Please step out of those, you might fall over into the fire.' Trapped by her ankles, Laura stepped cautiously out of the jeans. 'You have wonderful ankles,' he said.

'Uncles, ankles.' (Faint memory of Clug.)

'What?'

'Nothing,' she said. (And who else?)

'Oh, Laura.' He pressed his face against her thighs, embracing them. 'Take off that great sweater.'

'Don't knock me over.' Laura sat down on the hearthrug. 'We could skip the reading,' she said, pulling the sweater over her head.

'Shall we? Here? By the fire?'

'Why not? It's comfortable, isn't it?' she said.

'Isn't it wonderful what arms, legs and hands can do, and mouths,' Claud said presently, lying with his mouth against her neck, her hair brushing his eyes. 'I could weep, I am so happy.' He felt the warmth of the fire on his back, contrasting it with the temperature of Laura's body. He could not see her face above his, frowning, puzzled, amused. 'I have thought so much about you all this long time.'

'And who else?' Laura questioned gently.

'Nobody else.'

'Mavis, for instance, or Susie?'

'Oh no. Nobody, unless you count the girl in the book.'

'Does she make love like this?'

'Of course. "These little deaths, this rare love." I cut that sentence. It was one of the first to go into the wastepaper basket. Oh God, Laura! I haven't given you my present. I left it at the corner of the house when I - what a fool I am! It's the proof that I—' Claud scrambled to his feet, rushed to the door, darted, naked as he was, out.

Laura sat up crossly, feeling the draught of icy air let in by Claud, and pulled her sweater over her head. She was reaching for her jeans when Claud returned.

'Christ, it's cold out there.' He was shivering. 'Here it is, my present, all for you.'

'Shut the door, Claud. What is it?' She took the plastic bag he handed her. 'Sit down, get warm, put another log on the fire. Let's have a look. Oh!'

'It is everything I have discarded, all the parings. No, you are not to read them. I brought them to you to prove that I have cut, cut, whittled down, cut, what's the word?'

'Edited?'

'Yes.'

'Shall we burn it, then?' She peered at the waste paper.

'Of course, that was my hope.'

'Not in here, it would set the chimney on fire. I know, let us put it on my bonfire. Put some clothes on, let's do it now.'

They dressed, laughing, excited, and hurried into the garden. Laura seized her rake and parted the bonfire, which flared up, crackled and spat in the darkness. Claud tipped the contents of the bag into its centre, then Laura raked the fire back, piling sticks and leaves high over the paper. They watched the smoke curl into the moonlight, heavy acrid smoke stifling the aromatic scent of the winter burning, making them cough and move away. Then, 'Leave it, come in, let us open a bottle of wine,' said Laura. 'We'll celebrate, find something to eat.'

'And then back to bed?'

'Why not?' She felt lighthearted, happy, rash.

As they opened the door the cat skittered out between their feet. Claud thought: Now we can have the bed. The cat disappeared, leaping.

Laura beat eggs for an omelette, mixed a salad, found bread and cheese. Claud opened a bottle of wine. As they ate he began telling her about his book, his thoughts pouring out in a rush, the plot unravelling between mouthfuls of omelette and gulps of wine. Sometimes he searched the meagre remains of his manuscript and read extracts which had escaped the holocaust. Laura listened, surprised, entranced, moved. At last, when the food was eaten, the wine drunk, the story told, she said very quietly, 'It's good, it's very good,' sighing, 'wonderful.'

'You mean that?' He was trembling.

'Yes, I do.'

'If it fails I shall never write another word. I shall kill myself.'

'There should be no such thought.' Laura was distressed.

'But there is, there would be.'

'You are exhausted, so am I. Come to bed.'

'Did you mean it? Do you really think – you just said it's good to comfort me, to console.' He was suspicious.

'I did not. It is good. If you write it as you told it and keep the bits you read to me, you cannot fail. I swear it's good.'

'You will not betray me?'

'What is there to betray? Of course I shan't, don't be stupid.'

'Swear—'

'Look, Claud, I am tired, so are you. What is this?'

'Fear of failure. Fear of death. Same thing. Laura. Promise me—'

Melodrama, thought Laura, sleepy by now. This reminds me of recent Clug. Why do I pick artists? 'Come to bed, darling. I promise to try not to betray. Will that do?'

'Why only try?' Claud was excited, excited by his book, by the bonfire, by love-making, by the wine. 'Give me half a promise then,' he shouted.

'I will give you that willingly.' She put her arms round him and held him close. 'I am only half a person,' she said.

'Laura, you are crying. Why do you cry?'

'It is the smoke from the bonfire.' She wiped the tears with her knuckles. I am flawed, she thought, I am in danger. 'Listen,' she said, 'listen to the night. Go to sleep.'

'I can hear your heart. Will you give it to me?'

'Not possible.'

'Will you marry me?'

'Don't make stupid jokes.'

'No joke, I repeat: will you marry me?'

'When I am seventy-five, you will be fifty-three.'

'So? Will you marry me?'

'I am old enough to be your mother. Go to sleep.' She rocked him gently in her arms, stroking him. What smooth and lovely flesh, how hard the muscles, how fine the flat stomach, ah, there and there, how straight the spine, what delicious nobs. 'Sleep now. Stop talking, listen to the night.'

'There's a gale getting up, the stillness moves.'

'Yes, yes, listen, lie quiet.'

'Tomorrow I shall start the book all over again.'

'Yes. The final version. Yes.'

She watched his face by the firelight flickering in the next room, saw him close his eyes, sleep, let go. She listened to the anxious rising wind as it gathered strength, thrashing up from the south-west, testing its strength on the trees until they groaned and winced. Claud shifted away from her, muttering and mumbling.

She slid from the bed and went to the window. Clouds raced now across the moon, drawing shadow patterns on the grass. The bonfire flared up, smoke beaten down drifted sideways. The little cat rushed suddenly across her line of vision, chasing, careering. The heart of the fire flared, broke open, exposing bits of paper which, catching the wind, escaped. Laura picked her clothes off the floor, tiptoed from the room, dressed, slipped warm feet into cold boots, let herself out into the windy garden. The wind was roaring now, hell-bent, savage. She ran stooping in the moonlight, catching sheets of typescript, stuffing them back into the fire, raking up the sides, dodging the smoke which, changing direction by the minute, caught her by the throat and sent her coughing back, tears streaming down her cheeks.

Months of work, she thought, watching it burn. Will he succeed, will he write what he told me tonight? It was so good, she thought, watching the fire, will he be able to write it down as he told it, sparse, passionate, original? The cat raced past, buffeting a ball of paper, tossing it in the air, snatching it with its paws, patting, waiting for the wind to startle it into flight so that she could creep, pounce and torment.

Laura bent down, snatched up the cat's toy, held it in her hand ready to toss back onto the fire, hesitated, smoothed out the crumpled sheet, read, peering close by the light of the moon. When she had read, she crushed the paper violently between her hands, crouched down by the bonfire, thrust deep into the heart of the fire, cried out in anguish as the fire scorched, sprang back, snatched up the rake and raked up the sides of the bonfire so that all that remained of the paper was totally covered.

Its game spoiled, the cat rejoined her as she let herself into the house. She bit her lip against the pain as she searched for Acriflex to cover the burn. Tears blurred her vision. Gasping a little she tended her wound, muttering to herself, 'You fool, you fool,' as she covered the burn with gauze. Then she squatted by the fire waiting for the pain to subside, for her equanimity to return. At last she stood up, went to the window, drew the curtains. It would soon be dawn. The wind, decreasing, stroked the branches it had savaged. The fire was almost burned out. There was only fitful smoke.

She felt very tired, consumed by the desire for sleep. She took cushions from the chairs, laid them on the hearthrug. In the bedroom Claud slept sprawled across her bed, his head thrown back, arms wide, breathing evenly. She took a blanket which had slipped to the floor and, closing the door, stretched out by the fire, covering herself with the blanket, laying her head on the cushions. The pain of the burn was less immediate. Her thoughts under control, she felt the cat creep up past her feet to settle purring by her head. The balance which had tipped was regained. Tomorrow she would care for Emily and Nicholas. As soon as they were well she would return to London to catch up with her orders, the boring awful hand for Helen's fake Apollo for instance. She would scramble back to normal. She fell asleep exhausted.

Laura woke to hear Claud moving about. She feigned sleep. She did not want to talk to him, needed time to recover her composure. She heard him dressing, muttering to himself as he did so. He came into her living-room and, seeing her lying on the hearthrug, whispered, 'Oh.' She waited for him to go. If she let him know she was awake he would expect breakfast and, worse still, conversation and love.

Claud knelt near her and added kindling then logs to

the dying fire. He did not touch her. She listened to him moving about the room, to the sound of paper torn from a pad, a pause while he wrote a message. Then he let himself out. She heard the scuffle as he put on his shoes. Then he was gone.

The slight draught from the briefly-opened door counterbalanced the fire which flared up, spitting, as the flame travelled. She was aware of her scorched hand. The burn was not a bad one; her hand had not been long in the fire. She felt uncomfortable from sleeping in her clothes, looked round the untidy room in disgust. Its deliberate chaos usually helped her endure her visits to her family, but not today. She decided that she would reduce her quarters to order before she returned to her obsessively neat flat. Standing chilly and dishevelled, she now keenly wished to get back to London but for a few days at best she must stay and care for Emily and Nicholas. She was ruefully amused by a sense of responsibility quite lacking in her parents.

Claud's note on the table said: 'Darling, sleep on. Am off to joyous work. I will come back tonight. Love C.'

'He is very sure of himself,' she said to the cat.

She ran a bath and as she soaked in the hot water composed a list of mundane things she must do. Finish tidying the garden, clean the house, create order in her disorderly rooms, persuade the cleaning lady to return as soon as her period of mourning was over, stock up Nicholas and Emily's store cupboards and deep-freeze, take their clothes to the cleaners, have their car serviced, make a blitz with the Hoover to rid carpets, sofas and chairs of Bonzo's hairs, and finally bath Bonzo. Making her list she cajoled her normal self to take over. She got out of the bath and dressed in bright yellow trousers, a pink shirt, green sweater. Her hand still pained her a bit, but it would heal. She would not forget what she had read on that ball of paper. She would make use of its memory to counterbalance her feelings (feelings which had been in danger of bolting up a blind alley). She would not stop sleeping with Claud just yet but the terms must be hers, as they had been at the beginning in the loft when she had been the sexual leader.

As she put a fresh dressing on her hand she grimly recalled unravelling the cat's toy, and reading what Claud had written. A passionate declaration, an explicit detailed description of love and not just physical love was stressed. There was a zest of the spiritual. (It was a fine piece of writing; she hoped he carried it in his head to write again.) From past experience she knew it was possible to cope with a live rival if so minded, it could be rather entertaining, but she recoiled from competition with a person as purely imaginary as Claud's girl May. (He had not last night quite got around to May; he had skated and glossed over her as he told his tale.) May, Laura thought, what an awful name. No drama about a name like May. Will May survive? Will he perhaps change May to some grander, more cogent, more dramatic name? The sheer silliness and inadequacy of the name eased her feelings, made her laugh, and feeling better so did her burned hand.

She tried to imagine May, a girl who was, after all, composite: Mavis' hair, Susie's skin, her own legs. It was absurd, laughable.

Then, remembering Claud's rendition of his book and how moved she had been, she dismissed these mean thoughts. Claud had created a girl who came alive, a girl who would linger in the minds of his readers, a person people would discuss, comparing her with other characters in literature. Like it or not May had style. I underestimated Claud, Laura thought. I used him for pleasure. I even suspected him of being a little camp. Then last night, serve me right, I went overboard, was even ridiculously in danger of believing his suggestion of marriage could be serious, not just froth. I could not have been much stupider than that.

Right then, Laura thought, I shall play second fiddle. Playing second fiddle to a fictional character has a certain originality. Having made this decision Laura was almost back to her old self.

Laura applied herself now to Nicholas and Emily; if she filled her days with their needs, she could keep her nights free for Claud. Past experience had taught her that one way of coping with complex feelings for her relations was to tidy their house; this somehow reduced them to manageable size. Out with the dust would go her guilt, and if like dust it reappeared that was the nature of things, though she always hoped there would somehow be less dust than before.

Finishing her attack on the garden, she planned what she would do to the house; there must be an awful lot of rubbish she could throw out. She would make life easier for Mrs Datchett when she came back. But first she tackled her own rooms. The organised chaos which had origins in adolescent protest no longer amused; she packed up cracked, chipped but valuable china for Claud's stall and replaced it with new things from Woolworths. She cleaned out cupboards, scrubbed, dusted and polished, reduced her possessions to a minimum. A lot of things went straight onto the bonfire. She excised objects of personal interest; the rooms must be functional, no more.

She had allowed too much to accumulate since building the brick partition; there must be as little left of her self as possible. The cat picked its way about the rearranged rooms in disgust but Claud, arriving each evening to eat supper, sit drinking by the fire before taking her to bed, was in such a state of euphoria over his book that he did not notice the changes. Laura was glad of this; it reduced his hold.

Hearing the sound of the Hoover Nicholas and Emily rose from their bed and, wrapped in dressing-gowns, looked down at Laura working in the hall. They were recovering from their flu but since the weather continued icy they prolonged their convalescence. Laura could look after them.

Emily said: 'Look at the dear girl, she is spring-cleaning. Were we as dirty as all that?'

'It's a sign of emotional disturbance, most *hausfraus* are neurotic. D'you think something has upset her?' joked her brother.

'Or somebody. Have you done the whole house?' Emily shouted above the hum of the machine.

'Almost. Bonzo has worked his hair into everything and it gathers in drifts in dark corners.' Laura looked up. 'Are you better?' she asked as the Hoover moaned to a stop. 'Have you taken your temperatures?'

'Normal,' said Emily. 'Come back to bed, Nicholas.'

'There's a parcel of books for you to review,' Laura called, 'if you want to read.'

'Bring them up when you bring our elevenses.' Nicholas trailed after Emily. 'When shall we tell her our plan?' he asked.

'Let her finish the cleaning. The last time she did this Mrs Datchett free-wheeled for weeks.' Emily switched on the television and lay back on her pillows to watch a programme on fashion. 'Look at those skirts, Nicholas, right up to their crotches!'

'There is a lot of banging and destruction going on downstairs,' Nicholas remarked, returning from a trip to the lavatory. 'She has the bit between her teeth. I trust she won't destroy anything precious. She is filling bin liners with all things unburnable.'

'Having a happy time. Did she bring up the books?'

'I fetched them. Shall we read and compose our reviews?'

'Let's see what there is.' Emily seized the parcel.

'She is burning Bonzo's old basket,' said Nicholas.

'He doesn't use that one any more.'

'And his blanket, probably thinks it full of fleas.'

'It probably is. Fleas' eggs last. Do you think she is making the house ready for the undertakers?'

'In which case we have a surprise for her, but no need to be morbid, Em. I say, let's have a look.' Nicholas reached for the books. 'I love the innocent smell of a new book. What shall we be this month, mean or charitable?'

'Let's damn with faint praise.' Emily relished their power. 'Oh, darling, you do look fierce, what's that sack for?' Emily clutched the duvet to her breast as Laura came into the room. 'What are you up to?'

'I am degenerating into a dutiful daughter,' said Laura lightly. 'Actually I am collecting empties to throw out, bottles, cartons, that sort of thing. Why do you never throw anything away? Look at all this.' She opened a cupboard. 'Gosh—'

'It might come in useful.'

'For what?' Laura snatched up paper, small boxes, empty tubes of toothpaste, old jars of face-cream and broken combs, dropping them into her sack.

'Mrs Datchett is going to be pleased if she ever comes back,' said Nicholas placatingly. 'Especially if she only wants to do light work. Sit down a minute, Laura, and talk to us.'

'When I've finished this. She is coming back. I have been to see her.' Laura continued her clearance. 'Don't worry. What's all this?'

'We have something to tell you,' said Nicholas.

'Let her finish her wave of destruction,' said Emily. 'Have you had a go at your part of the house, Laura?'

'Yes. That wasn't too bad. What are all these?' Laura sat back on her heels. 'What are they?' She sniffed at a box of empty bottles. 'They smell – er – funny.'

'There was a shortage of bottles in the war; one returned the empties to the barber. One did the same with Fortnum's jars,' said Nicholas. 'One didn't always keep up the impetus.'

'The war ended in 1945,' said Laura, still thoughtfully sniffing. 'This was hair oil,' she said, puzzled.

'Penhaligon's best. Has it kept its scent?'

'You have not used it for years and years—'

Laura held a bottle to her nose. 'Oh—'

'Stop sniffing like that, Laura. What's the matter?'

'I think I will get your elevenses.' Laura dropped the bottles into the sack. As she carried it downstairs she thought, It can't be. It's my nasty suspicious mind. She tipped the sack into the dustbin.

In the kitchen she filled the kettle to make coffee and washed her hands. It was so long ago, she thought, I may be wrong. I wish I was. Why did I not realise at the time? What good would it have done?

She remembered the party, Nicholas and Emily's birthday. Everybody drank too much. She remembered waking next morning, the smell on the pillow. Christopher had been at the party with his mother and father, good old Ned – but Ned used that stuff from Trumpers. She remembered it well, it was quite different from— Did anything happen? Nothing? Surely nothing. I'd know if it had, would – I – not? One does not forget smells or what might have—

It was at least twenty years ago. Laura washed her hands again, made the coffee, carried the tray upstairs. Halfway up the stairs she stopped as twenty years of suppressed memory snapped. She remembered waking in her bedroom. The door closing as Nicholas left the room. The smell of his hair on the pillow, the stickiness on her nightdress and inner thighs. A mistlethrush had been singing outside in an apple tree, as one was singing now. Had the birdsong unlocked her memory? Her head had been aching. It was clear now. Had she wept? She remembered her heart thumping as it thumped now. She had bathed, oh yes, she had bathed and later Emily had accused her of taking all the hot water. Plotted to kill Nicholas? Contemplated suicide? She had forced herself to forget, buried her terrible anger deep, an anger which welled up now almost choking her as she stood on the stairs gripping the tray.

In the garden a robin chirped up in the lilac bushes in contrapuntal harmony to the mistlethrush, just as it had then all those years ago.

She continued up the stairs.

'What was it you wanted to tell me?' She laid the tray across Emily's lap.

Emily pursed her mouth. Nicholas paced the room. Laura sat on the bed at Emily's feet. 'You look better,' she said, 'both of you. You have recovered from your flu.' It was less easy to like them when they were well. 'You look positively spry,' she said. 'What's the secret? What have you to tell me?' She watched Nicholas. 'Nicholas—' she began.

'What?'

'Nothing.' What would be the use of asking him if he remembered the incident of all those years ago? If he did and he habitually trolled beds, I would feel no different, no sadder than I do. I did not, thank God, get pregnant.

Nicholas was speaking. 'What did you say? Sorry, I missed—'

'You never listen,' Emily shouted in sudden exasperation.

'Hush, Em,' said Nicholas. 'I was saying, Laura darling, that we have decided to have a living-in couple to look after us—'

'What a good idea,' said Laura. 'Where will you put them?' (Is there such a thing as circular incest? She considered her own question in all its permutations.)

'Well, darling, since you are never there, we thought the flat at the back. We will knock down your joke wall, of course.'

'Of course,' said Laura. 'Is that what you wanted to tell me?' She suppressed a shiver.

'I don't like your tone of voice,' said Emily.

'It won't be worrying you for long, Mother.'

'But you will come and stay with us,' said Nicholas.

'There will be no reason to.' Laura kept her voice level.

'But you are Emily's child, she's your mother.'

'And what are you, Nicholas?' Laura asked. 'What are you to me?'

Nicholas did not reply.

'Your coffee is getting cold,' said Laura. 'Drink it up.'

'It would choke me.' Nicholas put the cup aside.

'Tell me this, Nicholas. When I was collecting those empty bottles just now did you, too, remember a party years ago?'

Nicholas stared at Laura.

If I were writing a book, thought Laura, I would write that his mouth is working but it isn't and I don't feel anything, no extra pain, nothing. 'I think I have stunned myself with housework,' she said. 'Of course I will get out of my bit of the house. You have no need of me, I have no need of you. It's a pity, but there, never mind.'

'We thought,' said Emily, 'that with your business in London, your flat wherever it is, and the men you live with whoever they are, that it is a terrible bore for you just to come down from a sense of duty.'

It is, thought Laura, but this time Nicholas begged me to come, said you were dying. 'Wolf, cry wolf,' she said. (Surely it is better to be facetious than to accuse?) 'Nicholas,' she said cruelly, 'what's the matter? You are looking funny.'

Nicholas stood with his back to the light, his hands clenched to fists in his dressing-gown pockets. She could see his black eyes reflecting her own. 'Is this happening to us?' he said, ignoring Emily. 'An ordinary family?'

'I hope no one will ever call us that,' protested Emily with her usual sharp spirit. 'We are too remarkable. What's the fuss about?' She looked from Laura to Nicholas. 'We only want your rooms for servants or whatever they like to be called these days. I suppose they will consider us ordinary. Am I missing something?' she asked. 'Some nuance?'

'No,' said Laura, exchanging a glance with Nicholas, 'I don't think you are missing anything.'

'A few days ago you said you loved us.' Nicholas ignored his sister.

'So I did.' Laura stood up. 'Finished your coffee?' she asked. 'I'll see to your lunch. I bought fish.'

'Laura.' Nicholas followed her out of the room.

'It's all right,' said Laura, 'nothing's changed.'

'Oh dear,' said Nicholas, 'oh dear, oh dear.'

Laura started down the stairs with the coffee tray. The cups rattled annoyingly in their saucers. Nicholas caught up with her in the hall. 'It would be such a gross betrayal if you said anything to—'

'Don't worry, Nicholas,' she said, 'I told you nothing has changed. Worse,' she said, pushing open the kitchen door, 'can't be worse.'

'That's what you think,' said Nicholas. 'Oh darling, I do love you.'

'And that's a pity too. Go back to Emily, Nicholas, go!'

I shall put this out of my mind, she thought, washing the cups at the sink. I shall walk over the hills this afternoon and exhaust myself. I shall come back and have supper with Claud and go to bed with him and if May is in bed with us, it bloody well can't be helped. At least I shall get those two old grey people out of my mind. 'And tomorrow,' she said to the cat, 'we shall go back to London and stay there.'

Laura sat in the wine bar. She was wearing a snuff-coloured skirt and a bitter chocolate jersey. At her feet in its wicker basket her small cat glowered.

Since she had been in in the autumn the bar had changed hands. The new owners kept it dark, compensating for the lack of light with soft musak and a line of rich *gâteaux* served with Viennese coffee, hoping to attract a classier clientèle than the market people who, with their loud talk and noisy camaraderie, had been apt to treat the bar as a club to the exclusion of others.

The market people had moved up the street to a new

establishment, Terrence informed Laura, which served sausages of all nationalities with a fine variety of pickles and mustards. 'They can make as much noise as they like there. You won't find people like Brian and Susie here any more. They've moved up the street, chips with everything.'

'When did this happen?' Laura sipped her wine.

'Last week.' Terrence idled by her table. 'I was offered a job there, but I've better things to do.'

'Oh?'

'I am going into private service. Would pussy like a saucer of milk?'

'No, thank you.' Laura looked up. Above the long apron, spotlessly clean, Terrence sported a striped waistcoat. 'I like the waistcoat.'

'My uncle brought it from Germany; some count's footman sold it to him. It's got his crest on the buttons.'

'Very nice. Shall you be happy in private service?'

'I mean to be.'

'Doesn't it depend on the people?'

'No problem, it's just an old couple.'

Terrence had grown taller during the winter, more robust. His face had filled out so that his teeth were less daunting. The probability occurred to Laura that the old couple might be Nicholas and Emily, that Nicholas and Emily might need protection, or conversely Terrence. But she was on her way to London. Nicholas, Emily and Terrence must fend for themselves. She raised her paper and pretended to read.

'I plan to get Mavis to work part-time with me,' said Terrence, ignoring the hint. 'It's a local job, see.'

'Very nice.' Laura folded the paper to the leader page. Was the thought of Terrence living in the rooms where she had made love to Claud abhorrent? She had been stupid to allow him to keep coming there; it would have been better to have stuck to the loft where somehow she had always kept the upper hand, contained her love (if that was what it was). If she had not had an assignation with Margaret Bannister she would have paid her bill and left.

'When I have some experience I shall go to a school for butlers and move on to the States. They pay terrific salaries there. You get your own car, the lot.'

'That's all right, then,' said Laura.

Terrence moved away to position himself by the bar, ready to swoop on customers as they came in.

He's a sly fellow, she thought. I've never much liked him. Why doesn't he say he is going to work for Nicholas and Emily? Perhaps he is not telling me because he resents my teasing him when Claud and I ate the oysters. Does he think I might put a damper on his plan? Will his smell obliterate the faint echo of Claud in my bed, of us lying by the fire? I must look on his presence in the Old Rectory not as a barrier but as a protective shield. I wonder how he will get on with Bonzo?

Laura looked at her watch. Unpunctual people irritated her; Margaret Bannister was late. She tapped a spoon against her empty glass, and gave Margaret another five minutes.

The street door swung open and Helen Peel came in. Laura raised her newspaper too late; Helen had seen her. 'When am I going to get my hand?' She advanced on Laura, sat without being asked at the table.

'Soon,' said Laura.

'I suppose you have been looking after Emily and Nicholas.' Helen always knew it all. 'They have had flu.'

'Yes.'

'She and Nicholas are bloody spoiled, never lift a finger, do they?'

'No.'

'I hear that they are going to have a living-in couple. Putting them in your part of the house. I suppose you know all this?'

'Yes.'

'Can't imagine how they can afford it, they must be living on capital. Aren't you worried?'

'No.'

'They can't make much from their articles and reviews.'

'No.'

'Where's that boy?' Helen snapped her fingers. 'Here, Terrence, stop picking your nose and bring me some coffee.'

'Yes, ma'am.' Terrence grovelled, 'Your usual chocolate gâteau with your coffee and whipped cream, ma'am?' He winked at Laura. 'Or will madam have wine today?'

'Coffee, of course. D'you suppose he's making fun of me? They normally call one love or ducks. What d'you think, Laura?'

'Yes.'

'Oh.' Helen looked surprised. Terrence set coffee, cream, and a large slice of cake before Helen. 'D'you think I should eat this? Christopher says I am losing my figure.'

'Lost.'

'You are a comic.' Helen laughed indulgently. 'Were you waiting for someone or do you want to be alone?' She examined the chocolate cake. 'What a large slice.'

'Yes.'

'You are not making yourself very agreeable.' Helen forked cake into her mouth. 'Monosyllabic as ever.'

'Cat got my tongue.' Laura leaned down, picked up

the cat basket and moved to go; as she did so Margaret Bannister came in, full of apologies. Laura led her to a table out of earshot of Helen. When she had ordered wine for Margaret, she said: 'I asked you to meet me so that I could give you this. It's money Claud made on his stall.'

'I don't—'

'It's my share of the stuff I gave him to start off with. You remember, a job lot from our attic? I thought of giving it to Oxfam, but I think if I give it to you to spend for Claud that would be best.'

'I don't understand.' Margaret looked suspiciously at the glass of wine Terrence placed before her, hesitated, then raised it to her lips, drank.

'Claud is writing a book, Margaret.' Laura turned her attention to Claud's mother. Claud had inherited her looks but was not yet as bruised by life. 'Claud is writing a book,' she repeated.

'I know that.' Margaret thought that she had never particularly liked Laura, or might not have liked her if she had ever got to know her well.

'It is going to be very good. He is in full flow and may not have time for his stall.'

'It's just a phase,' said Margaret dampingly.

'It may turn out to be a very long phase; he is extremely talented, Margaret.'

'Oh.' Margaret swallowed a mouthful of wine. 'How do you come into this?' Nothing irritated her more than being told about Claud, talented or otherwise, as though she were ignorant of his character. The more so since she suspected she was ignorant. 'Of course, he is talented,' she said.

'He read me a bit of his work the other day; I thought it wonderful,' said Laura. 'I am off to London,' she said reassuringly. 'I shan't be down here for ages.

I have not the time to give it him myself.'

'You could have posted it.' Margaret put the money in her bag. 'There was no need to make me come all this way from my new house. I am not living here any more, you know.'

Laura let this rudeness pass. She could not explain to Margaret her need to see her. She was not sure herself why she had desired the meeting. Was it part of her farewell to the neighbourhood? 'How is the new house?' she asked politely.

'I like it very much. I like the garden, the village is delightful, there is so much to do. Evening classes, lectures.' Margaret already regretted her rudeness, felt the need to give something to Laura. 'I can plan my days,' she said, 'without having to consider other people. Claud, for instance,' she smiled at Laura, 'and shades of my late husband.' She drank her wine. Perhaps she was giving too much? 'My new house has no memories. Perhaps you cannot understand that?' she said.

'I understand very well.' Laura signalled to Terrence to bring more wine. She thought of her London flat which held only herself. 'You have found freedom,' she said, 'for the first time since you married. You will turn feminist next, go soap-boxing.'

'You are making fun of me,' said Margaret, smiling. 'I can't think why I am talking to you like this. I hardly know you.'

'What else have you found?' Laura searched Margaret's face for traces of Claud. How would Claud use his mother in his writing? Did he know his mother? 'Tell me,' she said, 'what else?' She was surprised to find herself so interested.

'I have not stopped loving Claud or his father – but Claud—'

'You don't lose your maternal instinct just because you move house.'

'But you find a new perspective, see things differently!' Margaret wondered whether a childless person such as Laura could have maternal feelings.

'How so?'

'I am taking a course of psychology; when I finish I may be able to explain it better. To start with I have befriended someone who needs it. I feel maternal about him.'

'A young man?' This was interesting. 'A replacement?'

Margaret leaned closer to Laura. 'An old man,' she said, 'so lonely he flashed.'

'Like a glow worm?' Laura puzzled.

'No. His thing. To get attention. The only attention he got was passing the plate in church and that was negative. He is the most wonderful gardener. It wasn't sexual, it never is. He's like a child.'

'Second childhood? Very old?' Laura frowned.

'He can still dig an excellent trench.' Margaret spoke quite seriously.

Laura crowed with laughter. Margaret's substitute for Claud seemed totally out of character. 'What an amazing thing to do,' she said, 'it doesn't seem like you at all.'

'Why not? I was not much use to Claud.' Margaret spoke stiffly. 'Like any normal person I need something to keep me ticking. This poor old man will be the minimal replacement I can manage.' She drained her glass.

And I have no replacement. Laura sucked in her breath. Perhaps my empty heart will silt up, she thought, wishing now to get away. She signalled to Terrence to bring the bill, said that she must be off or she would get into a jam on the motorway. The brief moment of intimacy was over. She was anxious to leave.

They left the wine bar together. Laura waved at Helen, who shouted after her, 'Don't forget my hand,' so that other customers, looking puzzled, examined their own hands. Helen was gobbling a second slice of gâteau.

'I don't suppose she has a very happy life, in spite of Christopher Peel's money. All those statues must mean something. Perhaps they represent the beautiful people she had hoped her two boring children would be, and are not? My evening course on psychology may explain that too. It's amazing what one learns.' Margaret had now changed, or half-changed, or was prepared to change her opinion of Laura, would have liked to prolong the meeting, have another glass of wine, get a little drunker.

'Well,' said Laura, 'maybe.' She did not wish to discuss psychology. 'Thank you for meeting me. And for taking charge of the money.'

'See you soon, perhaps?' suggested Margaret. It would be nice to be friends with someone who thought so highly of Claud, someone who seemed to understand what you said.

'Not for a long, long time. My mother is getting a housekeeper, she will have no need of my visits.'

'Ah.' They walked along the street to Laura's car. Margaret now wondered whether she was not relieved that Laura would not be around? There were a lot of things she would like to ask, though. What sort of life did she lead in London? How did she manage? How did she know that Claud had talent? What made her so sure? What was Claud like in bed? She was sure Laura had been to bed with him. She did not give the impression that her sex life was ended; did she have a lover in London? What was it like for a young man of twenty-three with a woman of forty-five? Or for a woman of forty-five with a young man of twenty-three?'

'It must be nice,' she said.

'What?'

Margaret said, 'Nothing,' but she thought rather wistfully that Laura was getting something much more enjoyable with Claud than what she had experienced with Claud's father. 'He was so often drunk,' she muttered, and hoped Laura had not heard; she should not have drunk so much wine.

'Here is my car,' said Laura, who had heard and would presently ponder on the risks of amateur psychologists. She put the cat basket on the back seat.

'Will he find a publisher?' When Margaret was anxious, she looked like Claud.

'I am sure he will.'

'Will you find him one?'

'Claud's work has nothing to do with me, Margaret, you must know that.'

'It's true that he used to say that writing was what he wanted to do.'

'Well, then—'

'There were times when he was sulky and unpleasant.' In her mind Claud's mother multiplied the one scene with Claud into many.

'Now he is doing what he wants, he is happy, he will change.'

'You don't know much about psychology.'

'Maybe not. Well, goodbye. I must be off.' Laura kissed Margaret's cheek. She got into her car. Margaret walked ahead along the street. From behind she resembled Claud. It was something about the hunch of her shoulders, the length of stride.

Margaret stopped to look in a shop window, hesitated, went in. It would be easier to forget Margaret than her son. What a strange woman, Laura thought with amusement, withdrawing from her own child. How could she do it? And withdrawing deciding to ration out her affection on some old pervert, as though affection (love, if you like) were a commodity like the vegetables Brian and Susie weighed out in the market. But she would not stop loving Claud, Laura thought jealously, she had no need to. She was settling down, if she but knew, to the enjoyment of her maternity. Lucky Margaret, thought Laura, I cannot do that.

She switched on the ignition and pulled out into the street. Terrence, standing in the doorway of the wine bar, waved. 'Bloody cuckoo!' Laura shouted, but she returned the wave in case she should decide that she was grateful to him for filling the gap left at the Old Rectory.

'Bloody Nicholas and bloody Emily.' She changed gear to overtake a van and speed on her way out of town. 'They can't hold me any more. I shall fight free from the tentacles of conscience,' she shouted over her shoulder to the cat imprisoned in its basket on the back seat. 'I,' she shouted, 'can ration my love for them.' Nicholas, Emily, Helen, Christopher, Margaret and insolent Terrence would be tucked away out of sight in the cubby-holes of her mind to be thought of occasionally with love or affection, just as she thought of the American professor, the Hungarian painter, and of Clug. The immediate problem was to reduce Claud to similar, manageable size, find a secure cubby-hole for him.

Laura stopped to buy petrol, have her oil and tyres checked.

Had the djinn escaped from the bottle? Who would help her get it back? Up to now she had always been able to control her emotions, always kept love affairs light-hearted, enjoyable and brief, aware of the inevitable soon-to-be-arrived-at parting. (She had never permitted any suggestion of continuity.) She had kept a sloppy timetable with Claud, visiting him too often in the loft and lately allowing him to visit her every night in the Old Rectory. She had not toyed with love, not stopped when she still could have without pain.

And above all there had not been enough jokes. Jokes were the essence. Claud took everything seriously, he did not for instance compare well with Clug in that field.

Laura circled out onto the main road and increased speed. She had been in danger of losing her grip, she told herself irritably, and trod hard on the accelerator.

As she drove she savoured her last night with Claud. He had been caring and passionate, he had made love better than ever before, she had been physically and emotionally delighted, their union had been excellently synchronised, she could not fault it.

She had been a little puzzled by this notable success, she remembered now, until Claud, lying spent, his head on her breast, had volunteered that the last difficulty, the last tiny hitch in the composition of his novel was overcome.

'And what was it?' She had stroked his throat with her finger. 'This awful hitch?'

'My girl's name, of course,' he had answered sharply.

'Oh?' she had asked sleepy, relaxed, content.

'May will not do at all.'

'No?'

'Her name, of course, is Lydia.'

'Of course. Excellent.'

'She still has your legs.'

She had not noticed help was at hand.

Laura, braking carefully, glancing cautiously in her rear mirror, drew into a lay-by and switched off the engine.

A man driving past said worriedly to his passenger, 'Do you think that woman is all right? Should we stop and help? Phone at the next phone booth? She is hooting with laughter.'

After wiping her eyes, Laura thought delightedly of Lydia, that thanks to her she was free. She was no longer even second fiddle. All the way up to London she let off little snuffles and spurts of affectionate healing laughter.

PART III

A Year Later

A year later, if she thought of Claud, it seemed right to Laura that an affair begun in a spirit of jest should end on the same note. Her life in London was so remote from the atmosphere of the Old Rectory and the tightly interlocking society of the country town that it had been relatively easy to let thoughts of Claud dwindle to manageable proportions. If she had been in danger of making herself ridiculous, she was the only person to be aware of it.

Her work kept her busy; she made several trips abroad, going twice to Brussels, once to Milan, and once to Lyons. She went on holiday as she had often before to stay with hospitable friends in Tuscany, where she dallied agreeably with a fellow guest who was at a loose end between divorces. She found his company relaxing and enjoyable. Reminded briefly of Claud as she straddled her new acquaintance, she thought how much easier it was to be agreeable to people who made no demands, were not intense.

Every two or three months she telephoned her mother (a duty call). She learned that life at the Old Rectory carried on much as usual. The acquisition of living-in help had not made much difference. For reasons of her own Emily was for some time coy about naming her minions, letting slip only by degrees that the live-in housekeeper was Terrence and his aide, Mavis, who lent a hand when she felt like it.

It transpired that Emily had hoped that Mavis would couple up with Terrence, but Nicholas thought Terrence was homosexual, which knocked that little plan on the head. Fortunately Bonzo had taken to both the young people.

Laura did not speak to Nicholas.

On her return from one of her business trips there had been a letter from Claud forwarded from the Old Rectory. He asked her to meet him for lunch on a day already past to celebrate the acceptance of his book by a publisher.

Laura had not (being so splendidly distanced) even known that the book was finished. She had presently dialled Ann Kennedy's number. Ann answered.

'Yes,' Ann had said. Claud's book was to be published; he was getting a good advance. He had been to London to meet with his editor. Happily Mavis had been home – yes, resting – she had gone with him to see the editor to give moral support. He had been nervous, poor boy.

'How fortunate,' said Laura, 'for Claud.' Was Mavis filling the gap? Was Mavis' precious virginity at risk? Would she, Laura, mind a Mavis/Claud linkage or Mavis' virginity kept or lost? Neither eventuality moved her in the slightest.

Ann said she would tell Claud to ring Laura when he came in from the market. Claud was making rather a good thing out of his stall, quite a respectable amount of money. Mavis gave him a hand sometimes.

Laura noted with amusement the change in Ann. Claud, no longer in need of bolstering by his mother, was earning real money.

When later Claud telephoned, Laura asked, 'How

did you get my number?'

'I braved your mother. That terrible dog tried to bite me.'

'All you have to do is shout, "Die for Eastbourne". He isn't really ferocious. Tell me about your book. I am so pleased. So happy for you. I told you it was good, didn't I?'

'You did, you did.'

'When is publication?'

'May.'

'I can't wait for the reviews.'

'If I get bad reviews I shall kill myself.'

'Don't start that again, start a new book.'

'I have.'

'Oh, good. What is this one about?'

'It's a sequel to *Lydia*. Surely, I told you my novel is called *Lydia*?'

'No.'

'Well, it is. Wonderful title, isn't it? If you create a character as I have with Lydia, you can write a series. My editor is all in favour.'

'Oh.'

'I scrapped all that crap about machines and my mother and the girl wearing her Walkman, you knew that?'

'No.'

'I'm sure I told you.'

'Does she, Lydia, still have—'

'Your legs. Well, yes. I can't scrap your legs, they are an integral part. And Mavis' hair, of course.'

'Susie's skin?'

'I've let Susie's skin lapse.'

'Oh, why?'

'Well that carry on with—'

'Drinking her pee?'

'It's not really on, is it?'

'It's your book.'

'Oh, Laura, I am working terrifically hard; the book, the new one, is flowing. When I get my advance I shall invest in a word processor.'

'My, my. Shall you move out of the loft?' She could not visualise a word processor in the loft, it was far too grand.

'If the book gets good reviews I shall move, but until I'm sure—'

'You will get good reviews.'

'Promise?'

Laura crossed her fingers. 'I am sure you will.'

'Mavis wants me to write television scripts for her.'

'Does she indeed.'

'She thinks my dialogue is very good.'

'Really?'

'I incorporate a lot I overhear in the market into my work.'

'Is that so?'

'What is so, Laura, is that I shall badly need you around when those reviews come along.'

'As an integral somebody?'

'Laura!'

'A joke, Claud.'

'But you will be there?'

'In some capacity.'

'Wonderful.'

Putting the receiver back in its cradle, Laura thought that of all the people down there in the country the only one she missed was Bonzo.

Claud walked along the street in a state of elation. The sun shone. At breakfast in Ann's kitchen he had read the review of his novel, *Lydia*. His first review.

The words sensitive, witty, stylish, percipient, talented, waltzed through his brain. He was happy in a way he had never been happy before.

He was an author bursting onto the literary scene. *Lydia* was welcomed in print, the arts critic of a prestigious newspaper had generously praised his book. Happiness! His editor had telephoned him from his home before leaving for the office. Congratulations!

The bookshop had three copies on display in the window. 'Local author.' Claud went into the shop. He needed the excuse yet again to feel the book, sniff its newness, the special smell of an unread book, see the photograph of himself on the back, read the blurb (which he knew by heart), approve once more of the jacket (rather eyecatching and startling), discuss the pillar-box red binding.

Had the shop seen the review? Indeed yes, wasn't it good? Now we must wait for the Sundays. Would he like to sign the copies in stock? Of course. Claud signed, laughed joyously, exchanged pleasantries, did not quite dare to ask if they would order more than these three—

He continued on his way. Ann had asked him to call at the fruit shop since he was too excited to work, and buy her six bananas and two pounds of Cox's apples, here's the money, no doubt she would soon be seeing him on television. (It was a pity she never read a book.) Passing the newsagent Claud bought two more copies of the paper. He would send a cutting to his mother, who only read *The Guardian*, and keep one for himself. Mavis had said he must keep a cuttings book. He was to meet Mavis in the wine bar to celebrate. It was lovely to sit at a table with Mavis. People commented audibly on her looks, the colour of her hair. Today, with luck, they would point him out to each other as a writer (if not today, they would soon). Alas that Terrence would not be there to wait on them. Since discovering Claud had written a novel that was about to be published, Terrence affected to have read Proust. Let him now read *Lydia*, but his own copy.

Carrying Ann's bananas and apples, the extra copies of the newspaper, and his happy head high, Claud continued on his way, running into Nicholas and Emily outside the post office.

'Hullo,' said Nicholas, 'our local author.'

'Hullo,' said Emily, 'felicitations.'

'Hullo,' said Claud, exploding with smiles. 'Have you seen the marvellous review of my book in *The Times*?'

Nicholas looked unusually intelligent. Emily smiled slyly. 'Nicholas Shakespeare is so kind,' she said.

In London on the bus, on her way to her workshop, Laura also read the review. By coincidence it shared among others on the arts page a preview of a series of concerts to be conducted by Clug the following autumn. It was a long time ago that he had conducted at the charity concert where she had met Claud. He had grown greatly in international stature since and Claud had become a writer. To pick up where one had left off was as far from Clug's mode as her own. He would not, she thought, be sending her free tickets.

She was mildly irritated that her feelings for Claud were not as dispassionate as those she held for Clug. It would be churlish, though, to put off congratulating him. When she reached her studio she dialled Ann Kennedy's number and asked for Claud.

'He is out,' said Ann. 'I can give him a message.

Shall I do that or will you ring again later? He is celebrating with Mavis.'

'Just give him my congratulations, tell him how happy I am for him.'

'Will do,' said Ann.

As she worked Laura found herself worrying as to what Nicholas and Emily would say about Claud's novel. During the pre-publication months it had occurred to her several times to suggest that they should give the book a puff, but on mature thought she had decided that such a move would invite mischief; she rather hoped that *Lydia* would escape their notice.

During her lunch break she went out and bought a copy of a weekly Nicholas wrote for and a copy of the woman's magazine which occasionally employed Emily. She scanned the reviews on Claud's behalf with some trepidation. *Lydia* had not escaped their notice.

Nicholas praised the book highly but briefly. 'A brilliant first novel.'

Emily's piece was longer. While damning with faint praise, 'Claud Bannister is a witty leg-fetishist,' Emily hedged her bets by using expressions such as 'for discerning readers' and 'a good read to tuck up with'; her one-and-a-half paragraphs might, probably would, be construed by the charitably-minded as a recommendation.

Laura was relieved for Claud; they could have done so much worse. It was pretty safe to expect kindness from the Sundays.

She had promised to stand by, but she did not think he would need her support. She would not telephone. She would write a thoughtful, affectionate, congratulatory letter.

She supposed that there would be a word processor now and that he would move out of the loft. Would *Lydia*'s successor keep the same style of legs?

How nice to be a writer, thought Laura, to kill off, alter, or totally transform a character as Claud had transformed Amy and not have to wait as lesser mortals such as herself for time to dull recollection.

When she found the parcel containing the hand for Helen Peel's Apollo hidden under a stack of out-of-date telephone directories, Laura felt a fool.

The parcel should have been posted at least a year before. If anyone had asked her she would have sworn that she had despatched it; she had even, when doing her annual accounts for the income tax, thought that Helen was more than usually dilatory in not sending a cheque.

Since the fabric of her life depended on meticulous attention to detail Laura was shaken. She wondered whether this unconscious act of self-sabotage might not indicate that she was starting the menopause. She had long since decided to be sensible about the menopause, but if it did things like this to her it would play ducks and drakes with her well-ordered existence.

Continuing with the annual clearance of her workshop, a practice she normally enjoyed, she found herself irrationally cursing Helen for not reminding her, for not sending Christopher to harass her, for letting her forget. She remembered now that when she had last seen Helen, Helen had reminded her, a reminder that she instantly forgot since her thoughts had been busy with Claud. There had been far too much thought of Claud, she told herself angrily. He had lasted too long in the first place and he was now only having a come-back thanks to his novel.

Laura threw the telephone directories into the bin. Damn Claud, she thought, slamming the lid on the bin. She would take the hand down to Helen during the coming week, grovel, fix the hand onto the god for her, tell her not to worry about the bill. Helen would be embarrassed and she, Laura, would feel better. This really is menopausal stuff, she thought.

Having fixed Helen, she would call in on Nicholas and Emily for a surprise visit. There would be no time to see Claud. He had moved on in his life, as she had in hers; thoughts of Claud were retrogressive; she never bothered to think of Clug or other lovers like this; it was nice to meet them occasionally on a friendly basis, but they were 'over', were they not?

She finished cleaning the workshop, looked round at the order she had reduced it to with satisfaction and left.

That afternoon she walked through the parks to Trafalgar Square, spent an hour in the National Gallery, had dinner with friends and went to bed. The following day being Sunday she would sleep late as she usually did, wander out to buy the papers and, depending on the weather, decide how to spend her day.

In the event she was wakened early by some American friends she had not seen for over a year, who drove her down to spend the day near Oxford. When she got home, it was late. She was tired and rolled into bed after feeding the cat without bothering to listen to possible messages on the Ansaphone.

It was Monday evening before she thought to bother about messages. She had had an unexpectedly busy day; clients with urgent orders from abroad had kept her late at work. She was tired when she reached her flat, had a leisurely bath, washed her hair, changed her clothes, poured herself a stiff drink of whisky, put her feet up on the sofa and switched on the Ansaphone.

The first two messages were routine; she sipped her drink. Then there was a blank, then a loud screechy voice which she did not recognise started an incoherent babble about not knowing what to do and would she come at once. A second voice interrupted, 'Here Mum, let me,' and 'We got your number from your mother, Laura, what an old bitch, can you come, it's about Claud, he's—'

'No,' said the first voice very loud this time. 'Tell her what he is doing, he—'

Laura placed the voices as those of Ann and Mavis.

'He's not doing anything,' said Mavis' voice.

'I hate these machines,' Ann squeaked. 'He might kill himself, Laura, he won't talk to anyone, his mother is coming.'

There was a pause, then, 'Mavis, d'you think this will reach her? Shouldn't we call the—' Laura gulped a mouthful of whisky. The machine was still running.

'Laura Thornby is not here at the moment,' it said in Laura's voice, 'but if you care to leave a message, she will get back to you as soon as she can.'

'I am sorry to bother you,' said Margaret Bannister's voice, 'but Claud is behaving very oddly; he has shut himself up there and—' Here the voice which had begun calmly choked. Mavis took over, excited, almost laughing. 'Mrs Bannister says his father was a manic depressive.'

'No, I said he was an alcoholic; any psychologist will tell you that an alcoholic is not necessarily a manic depressive, though sometimes—' Margaret sounded cross and assertive. The machine clicked, then repeated, 'Laura Thornby is not here at the moment, but if you care to leave a message, she will get back to you as soon as she can.' Then a man's voice asked whether she was in a position to come and measure up for a foot repair on a statue on a fountain in Tewkesbury recently damaged by vandals. A letter with full particulars would follow, thank you.

Laura took another gulp of whisky, looked up Ann Kennedy's number and dialled. 'Hullo,' said a masculine voice.

'Ann Kennedy, please,' said Laura. 'This is Laura Thornby.'

'You'd better talk to Mavis,' said the man.

'Who are you?' asked Laura.

'Laura?' Mavis came on the line. 'At *last*!'

'What the hell is going on?' asked Laura.

'We have been trying to reach you ever since yesterday,' said Mavis, gasping. 'Claud's gone bananas.'

'What's—'

'It's the Sunday papers.'

'What?'

'The reviews! Claud's book! Haven't you read them, don't say you missed—'

'No.'

'Oh!'

'What do they say?'

Mavis let out a sound between a giggle and a shriek. 'I'll let Martin read it. I just double up every time, it's so funny. Here he is.'

The masculine voice said, 'It's only one review. Shall I read it to you?'

'Please.'

'It's quite long, I'll pick out the offending bits. Here goes. It says, "Even the most average of readers deserves better than this", and um, here it says, "If there were a prize for the booby of the year, Claud Bannister's novel would win hands down", and here it remarks on "paragraphs overloaded with disintegrating vowels which would lie more happily in the WPB than on the printed page". He's having a ball, this reviewer.'

'What is really happening?' Laura took what she recognised would be Claud's mother's definition of a tight grip. 'Is it serious?'

'Hard to tell. I don't know the man. I gather he was psyched up, all joy over his reviews, very very happy, then yesterday morning this. He shut himself up up there and won't come out.'

'Ah.'

'Making a meal of it.'

'Oh.'

'Wants to see you though, shouted something to that effect to Mavis.'

'Is his mother there?'

'She was, but she went home, said his father did this sometimes. Brave lady.'

Laura did not know what to make of this.

'I'd say it would be a good idea if you could manage to come down,' said the man quietly.

'Not a laughing matter? Mavis sounds—'

'No,' said the man. 'No laughs.'

'I'll be there in an hour and a half,' said Laura.

Traffic was still pouring out of London onto the motorway; it would be rash to hurry. On the back seat the cat mewed in her basket, annoyed by the interruption to her routine. Laura found herself gripping the wheel unnecessarily tight as her mood swung between anger and fear. Why should she feel responsible? What was there to be afraid of? She was guilty of encouraging Claud to write. What was injured pride doing to him? Was he not an upper and downer, had she not on first meeting him called him Otis?

Overtaking a car she gave herself a fright by passing too close, nearly hitting it; the driver blasted his horn. Laura broke into a sweat. She should not have drunk such a strong whisky.

When she walked into the Kennedy kitchen, she said, 'Well? What's happening, what's going on?' aggressive from nerves. Ann, Mavis and Margaret Bannister were sitting round the table. A man she vaguely recognised but could not place leaned against the wall.

Ann Kennedy said, 'You are responsible for putting Claud in my loft, you get him out of it.' She was belligerent, her normal easy temperament in abeyance. Laura braced herself for a statement that the house was respectable, but Ann said no more.

Mavis said: 'He's got a gun.' Her eyes were shining, thrilled.

Margaret Bannister said, 'I thought I'd better come back as you were coming down. He won't speak to me. This is all so ridiculous. He should have joined a proper profession with a pension to look forward to, not been encouraged to fan about in an attic.'

The three women stared at Laura, anxious, excited, accusing. Mavis emitted a little splutter of mirth. 'We thought we'd wait for you before sending for—' began Ann.

'Fire, ambulance, police,' chanted Mavis. Theatrical London had done marvels for Mavis' self-confidence.

'I'll go up,' said Laura.

'I will come with you,' said the man who had so far not contributed, and pushed himself away from the wall.

'This is Martin Bengough,' said Ann rather formally. 'He's a great help.'

'Hullo,' said Laura. She wanted to ask what Claud had said or done, whether he had threatened – she decided it would be a waste of time. 'Come on, then,' she said to Martin. 'I don't believe he has a gun,' she said, climbing the stairs. 'I feel sure he can't shoot.'

'That's good.'

'I know you, you were one of the people who used to shadow Clug.' She climbed on, hurrying.

'Yes,' said Martin, keeping up. 'I was. I've been in Washington since then.'

'He loved it,' said Laura, reaching the top landing. 'Here we are, he must have put something on the trap to weigh it down. There's no bolt. I suppose they tried?'

'Told them to bugger off or he'd throw himself out of the window.'

'I don't think he would care to do that—' She started up the ladder.

Martin stood below, looking up at her; she was wearing grey jeans and a black cotton jersey. She had admirable ankles. Clug had been right.

'He has weighted it with something. I shall have to ask you to help me heave, I'll give him a shout first. Claud,' she shouted, 'Claud? It's me, Laura.'

There was no reply.

'Come on,' said Laura, 'help me.' She swung sideways on the ladder so that Martin could join her. He put his left arm round her to balance and pushed up strongly with his right. A heavy weight on the trap-door shifted. 'And again,' panted Laura. Martin put his head down, stepped higher on the ladder and heaved. His mouth was full of Laura's hair; the trap shuddered and gave way. 'Let me go first,' he said, 'if he's got a gun.'

'Don't be stupid.' Laura climbed past him into the

loft, pushed aside a load of books which Claud had used to block their entry. Claud lay face down on the bed, fully clothed. There was a whisky bottle empty by the bed and an empty bottle of pills.

Laura found Claud's pulse; Martin opened the windows wide, then picked up the pill bottle. 'Nitrazepan,' he said, holding it to the light. 'Mrs A. Kennedy. Two to be taken at night.'

'I can feel his pulse,' said Laura. 'Help me roll him onto his side. He must have stolen them.'

Martin rolled Claud over, pulling one leg up in the recovery position. 'He is stinking drunk,' he said.

'And drugged?' Laura pushed up Claud's eyelids; she was not sure what she was looking for.

Martin said, 'I don't think these are killers.' He showed Laura the bottle.

'It's the combination,' she said. 'D'you think you could call a doctor? I'll stay here.'

'Half a mo,' said Martin, kneeling on the far side of the bed. 'What have we here?' He scrabbled under the bed. 'Look!' He held out a handful of pills. 'He spilled the pills. I don't suppose he swallowed more than one or two.' He smiled at Laura across Claud's body. 'My bet is he's just plain stoned.' He watched Laura with interest. Her face was grey and taut as she stared back at him. She said, 'Black coffee, d'you think?'

'I'll see to it.' He left her with Claud.

When he came back she had covered Claud with blankets and was sitting beside him, holding his hand.

'I told them downstairs the panic's over.' Martin poured a mug of coffee. 'Let's try him with this.' He heaved Claud up, propping him with pillows. 'Mavis seemed quite disappointed. Will you hold the cup?'

Martin held Claud, while Laura held the cup to his

lips. Claud mumbled something, belched, went back to sleep.

'No good,' said Laura, 'it might choke him.'

'Matter of time,' said Martin.

They resettled Claud on his side. 'I don't think a doctor is necessary,' said Martin.

'No,' said Laura. 'What did his mother say?'

'She says his father used to do this, it's hereditary. She's gone home again.'

'Didn't she want to see him?'

'Said not, something about other commitments.'

'I don't know why sensible people seem so heartless,' Laura exclaimed passionately. 'She is not a heartless woman.'

'Shall you be sensible?' Martin thought she looked ugly with fatigue and fear.

'I shall sit with him.' She was defensive.

'I wasn't suggesting you were sensible.'

'He might be sick.' She ignored his remark.

'So he might.' Martin smiled at her across Claud's body, then looked away. Claud began to snore.

'Were you in love with him?' Martin caught Laura's eye.

Laura flushed, then as he watched she grew very pale and thoughtful.

Below them in the house there were sounds of Mavis and her mother going to bed, doors opened and shut, the lavatory flushed. In the town a clock struck the hour. Martin wound his watch; the excitement was over.

'Everyone gets at least one very bad review,' said Martin.

'I should have warned him if I had been around,' Laura said.

'But you weren't.'

'No.'

Martin wandered about the loft. He picked up the books Claud had used to block their entry, replaced them on the shelf, moved to Claud's desk and began riffling through some typescript. 'This will be his next book—' He began to read.

'Leave it alone,' said Laura savagely, then, as Martin spun round startled, 'it will be all right when he has torn most of it up. It has to be sieved, largely forgotten.'

Martin observed her defensiveness, her intensity. 'Like life?'

'Yes, of course.'

'So you did love him?'

Laura did not answer but took her hand away from Claud and folded it with the other in her lap.

'And you feel guilty and think you have betrayed him, I suppose.'

'Guilt is a fact of life,' she said.

'And betrayal?'

'That, too. Actually,' said Laura conversationally, 'what triggered whatever my feelings may have been was my inability to share.'

'With Mavis?' Martin made a wild guess.

'With Lydia,' said Laura and began to laugh.

'Who is Lydia?' Martin saw that laughter became her, made her eyes glitter.

'Lydia is his girl, the heroine of his novel. She has Mavis' hair and did have Susie who sells organic vegetables in the market's skin. Actually he dropped Susie, he was never too keen on her recipe for beauty. Lydia is a composite girl.'

'Does she have anything of you?' Martin watched her.

'Some mention, I believe, of my legs.'

'Bravo! Her character, though, what of that?'

'She has the character to suit her creator.'

'Creator?' Martin's eyebrows queried the use of the word or Laura's intonation.

'A writer's use of Godwottery, if I can use that word in an explanatory sense. He is in love with her, she is his perfect woman, a woman who will never hurt him. But a critic has attacked her, hence this.' Laura gestured towards Claud. 'When Lydia is threatened, he reacts like a rabbit eating its young to conceal them from the enemy. Claud kills himself.'

'Not very successfully,' said Martin. 'Bit on the bogus side, something of a bosh shot I'd say.'

'Well, no,' Laura murmured. She leaned over Claud, peering into his face: 'Can't get it right first go, can he? It's like the first draft of his book,' she whispered. 'You stupid, stupid fool.'

Laura sat beside the bed keeping watch. Martin settled in the chair by the desk, his back to the window. She had shaded the light from Claud's face. Neither of them spoke.

Laura listened to Claud's breathing, deep and regular now with only the occasional snore; from time to time she felt his pulse. Time passed slowly. The town was asleep.

Martin watched Laura, remembering her with Clug, an attractive intelligent woman having a good time. It had been an uncomplex job; she had been easy to track in her brilliant colours. They had, he and the others, watched for the clothes rather than her face. They had learned not to be foxed by the muted colours she wore to work. Her face, which had lit with merriment when she explained Lydia to him, was again blotted with anxiety and fatigue with dark smudges under her eyes. She was very different to the woman he had addressed briefly, breaking the rule of anonymity, as he boarded the train to follow Clug and she, catching his joke, had blown him a kiss. She looked half-dead now, sitting there beside Claud, who had this weird obsession for an imaginary girl. On the other hand, was he too not verging on obsession over Laura? Might the Laura he guessed at not be as imaginary as Lydia?

He tried to gauge her attitude. She had been angry when she called Claud a fool, loverly almost. Would she, if the occasion required it, have given Claud mouth-to-mouth resuscitation? The thought of such an intimacy appalled him. He imagined her covering Claud's mouth with her own, inhaling and exhaling his sour, stale, whisky breath, and was utterly disgusted, closing his eyes to blot out the inner vision, rearing away from his thoughts. When he looked again, he was surprised to see that the moment of passion when she had called Claud a fool was superseded by what looked remarkably like boredom.

Still Laura showed no inclination to talk. Martin looked around seeking inspiration. He must get her to talk.

He noticed a list pinned above the desk, got up to read it. 'Here's a list of methods of suicide. Do you think it was long planned?' He brought the list to Laura.

'He threatened once or twice, as people do.' She took the list. 'It's all negative,' she said. 'He wasn't keen.'

'Perhaps he meant it, though.'

'I took it to be histrionics when he threatened.'

'As his mother did.'

'She is not an easy mother; I don't think he is an

easy son. She is probably right to go home. If she or Ann had been really worried, they would have sent for help.'

'They sent for you.'

'But not official help. I should think Mavis worked everybody up. They were not to know that he had got pills and whisky; they obviously under the drama thought he was making a scene, then sulking.'

'Which, in effect, he was.'

'Yes.'

Silence reasserted itself. Laura seemed content to sit with her thoughts, but Martin felt a strangling desperation, a longing to shout and yell at her. He had waited so long to get to know her. What was going on in her mind? They had been up here hours, the world would wake up soon, he would lose his chance. He must take a risk. He said: 'Do you think while we wait for young Claud to surface that you could pretend that you and I are alone in a compartment in a train?'

'Why?'

'On the assumption that strangers meeting in trains can speak intimately, since the odds are they are safe to speak the truth because they will never meet again.'

'If you are bored, you can push off, go home, I am quite all right.' (I do not need you, her voice implied.)

Martin ignored the snub. 'What do you say to my suggestion?' His tone indicated that she might be chicken.

'Intimacy is not my *genre*,' she said, yet the idea of the train appealed to her, it had an irresponsible attraction; perhaps this man would prove truthful. 'All right,' she said, 'I'm game.'

'Shall I begin? My name is Martin Bengough. My

job in this country, which incidentally I have just chucked, has been to follow people like your conductor friend Clug when they visit and see that they don't spy on military establishments and so forth, but stick to their allotted programmes.'

'Jolly boring.'

'Usually yes. With Clug one got music and the bonus of watching you.'

'And discovering that I am not a military establishment.'

'Exactly.'

'Still pretty dire.'

'My aunt Calypso Grant thinks it's disreputable.'

'A bit harsh. You have to live and as I remember there was more than one of you.'

'Twelve of us.'

'My, my! Twelve people to spy on poor little Cluggie! Is that what we pay taxes for? Gosh.' Martin winced. 'Sorry, go on.'

'I was enchanted by you. I wanted to get to know you. When I passed Clug on to the next fellow for the last time, I doubled back here, made use of a silly ploy. I pretended to have lost my umbrella. I had left it in the concert hall on purpose. The caretaker girl told me that your mother would have it; this was splendid, I was able to come to your house, a legitimate excuse. You had been out with your parents, had difficulty with them when you arrived back—'

'I remember. They were legless. You were most helpful. My mother bit you. She can be naughty.'

'I bear the scar,' said Martin.

'And you knew the password for Bonzo.'

'The caretaker girl had warned me that he was fierce, told me about the Eastbourne bit.' Laura laughed. Was she relaxing? 'There now, we have made a start on our train journey. Were you in love with Clug?' Martin asked.

'Lord, no.' Laura was amused.

'I rather thought not. You don't allow yourself to fall in love.' (He would not tell her that she had been watched at other times with other men.) 'But you do go in for pleasure, I believe. Nobody gets hurt.' Should he go on, or had he gone too far, too fast?

'And?' She gave nothing away.

'You strayed from your norm with this one.' He glanced at Claud. 'Got hurt, probably. Feel responsible for him, perhaps?'

Bloody man, thought Laura, blast him, it all comes back, the struggle of a year exposed. She snapped, 'What else?' (What other truths would he dare to present her with?)

'You never allowed yourself to marry or have children.' He watched her face.

This self-confessed spy was aware of Nicholas and Emily yet she rather liked his open face with its honest grey eyes. He should have the guts to go on with the idiot game he had started. She hoped he was capable of hurdling the difficulties, or was he craven? 'Is that all?' she asked.

'A précis.'

'And?'

'I hoped during the last year, which I have spent in the States, to forget you. When I got back I came down here looking for you. I have been and am obsessed by you.' (Was she listening?)

Between them on the bed Claud emitted a porcine snort. Laura, pushing her thick hair back with one hand, leaned forward to stare at Claud. She said, 'Yes?'

'I didn't expect to find you in these circumstances.'

'No?'

'Watching your ex-lover revive from a suicide attempt makes it rather harder to come out with a - an - er—'

'What?'

(An offer, a suggestion, a proposition? What had he to offer?) 'I thought you and I might—'

'What?'

'Love,' said Martin. The word spoken out loud threatened them both.

Laura shrank into herself, drawing her knees up, hunching her shoulders as though a weight threatened to crush her.

Martin thought: We have here two failures, hers and mine. Could two failures constitute one success?

Laura said: 'I would not suit you. I am emotionally parsimonious.'

'Must it be so?' Martin asked.

'I am only half a person,' Laura said gently, for he seemed an agreeable sort of man. Then she said: 'I don't think your train is getting us anywhere.' Then more firmly she said, 'I think I shall get off it now. I see no destination.' Then she said, 'Oh look - he is waking up.'

Claud had opened his eyes.

Claud, focusing on Laura, said, 'Laura!' in a surprised voice. 'Great!' and went back to sleep.

Martin thought Laura's relief tangible. Her shoulders relaxed, she sighed, smiled, shook herself. 'The longer he sleeps, the better,' she said. 'He's okay now.'

Martin felt he must recapture her attention. While Claud slept she had at least listened. He asked sourly, 'What happens when he finally surfaces?'

'Gallons of tea and aspirin, and a boiling bath with ammonia in it. Could you organise that?' She got to her feet. 'Lord, I am stiff.' She rubbed her knees, stretched.

'Why the hell should I? He is your lover.' Martin's rage bubbled up. 'Is that what you have been planning,' he shouted, 'while we have been sitting here? Why should I organise his bath? He's nothing to do with me, he's yours. I thought you were worrying whether he was going to die of alcoholic poisoning, that you were feeling remorse, minding about the stupid sod.'

'All right, don't run his bath,' said Laura equably. 'I was worried. I was thinking while we played trains and so on that it would not be too awful if he did die.' She had shed her concerned appearance. She looked as he had first seen her in Clug's company, relaxed, distant, self-contained and bloody attractive. Martin drew in his breath. 'I must tell Mavis – or perhaps you would, oh no, you won't, will you – to buy him another wastepaper basket, for he will destroy most of that.' Laura pointed to the typescript on the desk. 'Then he will carry on with his next book and life with Lydia. And it will be all to do again,' she said. 'Next time, next book, next rotten review, you'll see.'

'I shan't see, I shan't be here,' said Martin loudly.

Laura did not appear to hear. 'I shall apologise to Ann for lumbering her with such a dodgy lodger and she will defend him. She will make it clear that his behaviour is in some way my fault, that no good comes of an affair between a very young man and a woman old enough to be his mother, that I am to blame for this little caper. The same goes for Margaret. Oh,' Laura swept her hair back from her face with both hands as her voice sank to a whisper, 'I thought that if he should die, I would be free of him, but you can only get free of live people, that's what resuscitation is about.' She began to tremble.

Martin pushed her gently down on the edge of the bed and sat beside her.

They sat with their backs to Claud. Martin pretended not to see tears pouring from Laura's eyes, dripping off her chin onto the black cotton jersey. He took her hand and held it. He said, 'Let's get back on the train for a bit.'

'All right.' She leaned sideways away from him and wiped her face on the sheet. Claud might not have been there. She stopped crying.

Martin said, 'Did you seduce him or did he seduce you?' He was painfully jealous.

'I came up the ladder one day and got into bed with him. There was an element of surprise. It's getting light outside, look, little pinkish clouds.'

'Go on.'

'I wanted to teach him how to make love. So many men never learn.'

'You did that?' Martin held her hand (it would not be difficult to put a pillow over Claud's head and hold it there).

'Yes. Listen, the birds are beginning to sing.'

'Then what?' (Better to let the bastard live.)

'Then I found it was not all talk and sex, he could write. It was so good, I helped him burn the first draft. I got burned myself.' She held her free hand up and turned it about. 'There's a scar somewhere.'

'There will be.'

'Then he fell in love with his girl. He truly loves her, she is part of him. He said if he got bad reviews, he would kill himself, suicide threats, tiresome emotional blackmail. Sitting here all night I have been thinking he's a selfish bastard. It would not matter if he did die. I was so angry I almost wanted him to. I knew he wouldn't, that he was merely stupefied with whisky and there was Lydia absolutely alive and perfectly sober.'

'Were you perhaps feeling guilty for seducing him?'

'No! We had a lovely time. How could I feel guilty about that? Wishing him dead, which I did for other reasons, is betrayal, though.'

'I wish,' said Martin, 'that you would give me the chance of betraying you.'

Laura looked astonished. 'Why?'

'You haven't taken in a word I said,' Martin yelled. 'I love you, I want you. I want to stop you wasting yourself on this ass.' He glanced contemptuously over his shoulder at Claud.

'But I have,' said Laura. 'I thought that was obvious. All I have had this night is a small hiccup of responsibility.'

'I thought you were torn in two.'

'It isn't being torn in two that matters, it's being shredded into little pieces so that you can never get back together, that matters.'

'And you are back together?'

'Yes. I am.' She seemed wonderfully calm now, cheerful.

'What about me? Give me a chance to love and betray,' (or play the clown) 'please.'

'No chance. I am getting off your train.' She was friendly, cheerful, composed. Perhaps he had not seen her weep? She was slipping away from him, he had never held her. 'Listen to the birds,' she said. 'It's time for me to be off.'

'God! I feel awful! Woeful, oh,' cried Claud. 'Ouch! I feel terrible.'

Laura leaned over Claud. Suddenly exasperated, she said: 'I bet you do. Listen to this, Claud. You have written a bloody good book, stop whingeing about one idiotic review and get on with the next. Tear up what you have written so far. Got that?'

Claud nodded and, since nodding hurt his head, groaned.

Laura stretched her arms above her head. 'Right, then. I'll send Mavis up with tea. If she's not awake she should be.' She moved to the trap-door. Martin followed her. She started down the ladder. 'Goodbye, Claud,' she shouted, 'goodbye.' She jumped the last yard of ladder and began running down the stairs. 'Wake up, Mavis.' She banged on Mavis' door. 'Wake up, it's over to you.'

Martin could hardly keep up, she ran fast, leaping two steps at a time. 'See Mavis swamps him with tea,' she shouted over her shoulder, 'and get aspirin from Ann.' She had reached the hall and was fumbling with the latch, opening the front door. 'Dear God!' she cried, 'I forgot my cat was in the car. How could I have forgotten her? Oh, puss, you have made a mess and no wonder, who could blame you?' She let the cat out of its basket and tipped the contents into the gutter. 'Oh, hell and damnation!' she exclaimed. 'It can't be true! I left Helen's Apollo's hand in London. I shall have to post it.' Then, noticing Martin standing at a loss, she snapped, 'Why have you not put the kettle on? Claud is dehydrated, he needs tea.'

'He can wait another few minutes. Where are you going?' Martin raised his voice. He was thirsty and tired by the long watch, desperate.

'Back to London. He needs tea,' Laura reiterated.

'Fuck his tea.'

'Oh!' Laura began to laugh. 'Oh-ho-ho-ho-ho.'

Martin caught her wrist. 'There's a delightful restaurant about ten miles from here in an old watermill. There's a stream. Will you come there with me? We could have breakfast?'

She freed her wrist. 'I got off that train,' she said. 'Go on, put the kettle on, he's dehydrated.'

Martin watched her car dwindle down the street. He thought, I shall not go on with this, as though the decision to part company was his. There was nothing to build on except imagination.

THE END

Harnessing Peacocks

Mary Wesley

'Delightful, intelligent entertainment'
THOMAS HINDE, SUNDAY TELEGRAPH

Hebe listened in the darkness of the hall to a family conference. The stern hypocrisy of her grandfather is winning the day. He has summoned her three horsey sisters' successful husbands and they are discussing Hebe's unexpected pregnancy. The decision, unanimous, is that it be terminated. Hebe, dissenting, flees into the night.

Twelve summers later she is living happily alone with her son in a seaside town in Cornwall. He is receiving an expensive education. Hebe has organised her life oddly but well. She has two chief talents in life – cooking and making love – and these she has exercised with dignity, in privacy and for profit.

It is when the separate strands of the web of Hebe's life become entangled that the even tenor of her days is threatened, and her life is changed.

HARNESSING PEACOCKS, Mary Wesley's third novel, is suffused with freshness, warmth and wit. The author's delightful literary skills are here fully engaged in a story of independence, honesty and sensual charm.

'Mary Wesley goes from strength to strength . . . She has a great zest for life . . . The book is tremendously lively, very funny, touching, spirited'
SUSAN HILL, GOOD HOUSEKEEPING

0 552 99210 0

BLACK SWAN